THE HELM
OF
DARKNESS

WAR ON THE
GODS
BOOK ONE

THE HELM
OF
DARKNESS

For the people out there going through a hard time
Who have been kicked down, who feel as though they have
nothing left in them
I just want you to know that yes, fate can be cruel
But you have a purpose on this planet
Whether it be as small as rescuing a classmate from a bully
Or as large as saving the world from pure evil
There's a reason you're here
Never give up.

CHAPTER ONE

STORM

Five hundred years in the future . . .

Summer, Year 500 AS

Syrena stood in the ruins of an old city, its roads reduced to rubble and craters. The buildings had crumbled long ago, and the sharp smell of pine reminded her of the forest towering along the perimeter of the debris.

The setting sun painted the blue sky with streaks of magenta, lavender, and peach. She smiled at the sight, remembering all the sunsets she'd watched with Spencer and Karter on the beach back home, then frowned. They weren't her friends anymore. They were her enemies.

Diana stepped up beside her and pushed her wavy blonde hair behind her ears. "Do you really think this will work?"

Syrena knit her brow, then pulled a dagger from her robes. "If it doesn't, I'm not sure the prophecy will ever come into effect." Pressing the cold blade against her wrist, she sucked in a sharp breath. "*When the world is taken back, and monsters rule the trees*"—she sliced her delicate olive skin with one swift movement, and blood trickled down her arm—"*blood of a demigod will spill. Two mortals will rise, two from the Before, reborn from sacrifice . . .*" She let the blood fall onto the debris.

For a while the two girls stood in silence, watching the blood drip from Syrena's arm, waiting for something, *anything* to happen.

But nothing did.

Tears filled Syrena's eyes, and she fell to her knees. After all they'd endured, after everything they'd done, how could this be happening? She'd broken rules, stolen pegasi and weapons, fought off monsters, and met with the Fates themselves to reach this moment. Even more than all that, she'd betrayed the gods. She'd left behind everything she'd ever known, just for her efforts to be rendered useless.

A loud squawk pierced the air, and she looked to the sky. Two creatures the size of chariots swooped down on them. They had the brown feathered bodies of birds, but from the neck up they were old human women with long gray hair, their wrinkled faces twisted in animosity.

Syrena's and Diana's two white pegasi neighed in panic, pulling at their restraints, and Diana drew her bow. "Zeus sent Harpies after us!" She shot arrow after arrow toward the bird women, but they dodged her attacks with incredible speed.

Syrena jumped to her feet, pulled out her pouch full of saltwater, and twirled her fingers above it. A familiar burst of pulsing hot power flooded her chest and arm. She brought her hand up, drawing the liquid out of the pouch in one fluid movement. The Harpies bolted above their heads and reached for them with sharp talons. Syrena lashed the Harpies' feet with her water as if it were a whip, and they howled, crashing into the ruins behind. Syrena waved her hand to draw the water back into her pouch, then swung around alongside Diana to face them.

The monsters climbed to their feet, ruffling their wings. "Stupid, stupid demigods," one said in a voice like old bones scraping against each other. "You missed your own execution."

Syrena's eyes widened, and she paused for a moment, looking down at her sliced wrist, blood still trickling from the wound. "*Two mortals will rise, two from the Before, reborn from sacrifice,*" she whispered to herself, smiling sadly as the realization hit her.

Diana sent more arrows soaring toward the Harpies, hitting one in the wing, while the other leapt out of the way and flew straight for Syrena. But she did nothing to protect herself. Instead, she stood still as stone, ready to embrace fate with open arms, ready to fulfill the prophecy.

The Harpy seized Syrena with its talons, the sharpened claws ripping through her dress and digging into her skin. Then she was in the air, the ground growing farther and farther away.

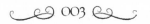

Below, Diana cried, "Syrena!" tears rolling down her freckled cheeks.

The sight made Syrena's chest ache, but she knew it was the only way. "It's up to you now, Diana!" she yelled. "It's up to you!"

* ~ * ~ * ~

Four years ago . . .

May 30th, 2014

The hospital monitor beeped slow and steady.

Andy's mom wept beside the bed, holding his dad's hand as the man lay in torment. Andy and his little sister, Melissa, sat together at the foot of the bed. Andy's gaze traveled around the stark white walls of the room, then finally fell on the dozens of tubes attached to his dad's body.

His dad was not well. He'd been sick for months, and his once-healthy frame had withered into a skeleton. Numerous silver strands popped up in his dark-brown hair with each passing day. His stormy gray eyes grew more dull and bloodshot every hour, his usually rosy cheeks a pale shade of yellow.

The sight of him made Andy's stomach sick.

"Kayla, if I don't make it, I promise you'll all be just fine," his dad croaked. "So long as you have each other." His mom broke into a new fit of sobs. His dad squeezed her hand, then looked to Andy and Melissa. "Come here, you two. Give your ol' man a hug, will you?" They didn't hesitate, resting their heads on his chest, avoiding his many tubes. He coughed, stroking their hair.

Andy didn't want his dad to die. He was only twelve—twelve-year-olds didn't lose their parents. It couldn't be his dad's time, not yet.

The hospital monitor began to shriek, and his mom shot up from her chair. "We need our nurse."

Within seconds, a trio of nurses burst into the hospital room and shoved Andy and Melissa off their dad. "We need all of you out, now," one of them said.

"I'm not leaving my husband," his mom said. She began to tremble and turned to face him. "Andy, please—take your sister out to the hall. Everything's going to be just fine."

Andy's chest tightened. He wanted to scream in protest; he wanted to stay with his dad. But he knew he needed to listen. He kissed his dad's hand, then pulled his sister into his arms and scurried out of the room. She screamed, pounding her tiny fists against his back. She was only four. She surely didn't understand what was happening.

"We need the doctor," a nurse said.

Andy collapsed outside the door and looked over his shoulder. The nurses worked over his dad, his mom standing at the edge of the room. As she watched them, she ripped out fistfuls of her black hair with shaking hands. Andy's eyes grew watery. He clutched his crying sister tight

against his chest, and hot tears streamed down his cheeks. "Dad," he said, choking on a sob. "Please don't leave us."

More hospital staff dashed into the room. "We're losing him!"

The monitor let out a long, solemn wail.

* ~ * ~ * ~

June 21st, 2014

Zoey walked into her mother's bedroom, so tiny it was like a shoebox. Lightning flashed outside the window. Rain and hail pummeled the glass. The room was barely illuminated by a lamp on the nightstand, which cast spooky shadows along the walls.

Zoey's mother stuffed the remainder of her clothes into a small suitcase at the foot of the bed. Why was she packing her things? They'd just moved into the apartment building a few months prior, days after Zoey's fourteenth birthday.

Her mother zipped up the bag, then narrowed her dark eyes at the floor and tucked a brown curl behind her ear. "Pack up, Zoey. We're leaving before they boot us out."

Zoey's heart sank. "What do you mean, 'before they boot us out'?"

"I mean exactly what I said. It'll be at the end of this week. Get your shit together."

Zoey's eyes filled with tears. "Are you out of money

again or something? What the hell? Where are we supposed to go?" Her mother said nothing, avoiding eye contact, and her chest grew tight. "Why don't you just let me live with Dad?" Zoey missed her father more than anything. She hadn't seen or heard from him since her parents' divorce.

Her mother balled her fists. "Your father doesn't want you."

Zoey shook her head and bolted down the hall, to the only other bedroom in the apartment. Her room. "I hate you! I want my dad!" She threw herself onto the bed.

Her mother stomped through the doorway, her footsteps booming. She snatched Zoey by her long brown hair and dragged her off the mattress. Zoey screamed. She flailed as she was yanked to the carpet, then slapped across the cheek. It stung worse than the time a wasp got her.

Her mother hit her again. And again. And again. She cried out, her body erupting with sharp pain, tears dripping down her cheeks into the fluffy carpet. She never remembered her father hitting her like that. She just wanted her father.

After what seemed like forever, her mother released her. Tiny beads of sweat rolled down the woman's wrinkled forehead. She grunted and exited the bedroom, leaving Zoey petrified on the floor.

A while back, there had been another time her mother couldn't afford to pay rent, at a different apartment complex. They'd had nowhere to go. No family to fall back on. For a few weeks, they'd been forced to live in their truck.

That was the last thing Zoey wanted to do.

Lightning flashed outside the window, temporarily lighting her empty bedroom walls. It faded as quickly as it came, and thunder rumbled, shaking the floor. A chill slithered up her spine.

She had an idea.

Perhaps *she* could pay the rent. Perhaps she could scrape up enough money by the end of the week, assuring they wouldn't have to live on the streets again.

But how? What could she do?

$$* \sim * \sim * \sim$$

Now . . .

November 15th, 2018

"This sucks," Andy said to his best friend, Mark, as their algebra teacher handed out midterm reports to the entire class. "I'm practically failing."

The classroom was tiny, with puke-green walls and zero air conditioning.

Mark fiddled with his pencil and flipped his pale-blond hair out of his eyes. "Maybe if you actually did your homework, you'd have better grades."

Andy groaned, crumpling his grade sheet. "Whatever. Remind me to come up with a reason my mom can't go to parent-teacher conferences."

The familiar voice of a girl said, "Mrs. Terry? Could I talk to you?" from behind, and Andy swung around to see Zoey Fawsen standing at the doorway of the classroom. She had curly brown hair that fell all the way down her back, tan skin, and eyes as blue as a clear summer sky. She was thin but still curvy, and around Andy's height. Her style was simple: lots of flannels, skinny jeans, and moccasins.

Andy had always thought she was gorgeous, and it took all his willpower not to stare. But he'd never talked to her. What if she thought he was a total weirdo?

Mrs. Terry smiled at Zoey and made her way to the back of the classroom to talk with her.

Mark rolled his eyes at Andy. "Try not to drool all over the table."

Andy snapped out of his trance, putting his head in his hands and glaring at his T-shirt. Two cartoon characters clashed swords on the wrinkled fabric, and he gave them a heavy sigh. Zoey would never notice a guy like him. He was scrawny and pale, chewed the tips of his thumbs every time he got nervous (which was a lot), and was barely passing many of his classes. His greatest talents were crushing the other players of every video game he played, and eating several boxes of stuffed-crust pineapple pizza all by himself without puking.

He adjusted his glasses. "Sorry. I can't help but stare at girls like that."

Mark patted him on the back. "The only girl I've ever seen you stare at like *that* is Zoey. But trust me, man, you don't want to get involved with her. She doesn't exactly have the best reputation."

He thought about the crazy stories regarding Zoey that had circled the school for the last few years. "You realize those are just rumors, right?"

The bell went off, high-pitched ringing bouncing off the walls, and the students gathered their things and bolted out the classroom door.

Andy and Mark made their way through the hordes of teenagers clustered in the hallways of their high school, and as they reached the commons area, a group of guys in muscle tees and sagging pants with chains hanging from their useless belts shoved them into a string of lockers. "Losers," they said, howling with laughter, then strutted down the hall as though they owned the school. Andy rolled his eyes. As if he cared what they thought of him.

Once they disappeared, Andy and Mark walked into the commons. Andy adjusted his backpack and pushed up his glasses. "Do you want me to drive you home?"

Mark shook his head. "Nah, man. I'm good. I'll just take the bus."

Andy shrugged. "Okay, see you later."

Mark waved, then turned and walked out the school entrance, while Andy started for the back doors leading to the junior parking lot. He whipped out his phone and called his mom.

"Hello?" she said.

Andy smiled. "Hey, Mom, I'm on my way home."

"Oh, of course, sweetheart. I'm picking up Melissa, but I'll see you when I get there." Her voice held a slight tremor.

"Mom, are you okay?"

"Yes, I'm just a little stressed because—"

Andy's phone was ripped from his hand and thrown across the school's commons. As it hit the floor, it shattered into tiny pieces. Other students huddled together in the commons burst into fits of laughter, and he whipped around to see who'd tossed the device.

Jet Weaver, a senior, gym rat, and giant asshole, towered over Andy at six feet tall. His shaggy blond hair hovered just above his icy-blue eyes, and his button-up and jeans looked perfectly fitted and ironed, as always. Probably because his mother was the store manager of a local clothing retailer, which Andy knew because his own mother happened to be one of the store's full-time employees.

Jet had harassed Andy since his mother started working there, around a year after his father died. The guy had some serious, deep-seated issues. It didn't seem like his parents paid much attention to him, so he bullied people until *they* paid him some attention, but Andy refused to let the taunting bother him. He didn't want to cause his mom any more trouble at work than she already had.

But if all that wasn't bad enough, Jet had dated probably every pretty girl his age in the entire city over the course of his high school career. Which, of course, included Zoey Fawsen.

Andy glared at Jet for a moment, peeved that he'd stooped so low as to destroy Andy's cell phone this time. Jet sneered and puffed his chest, and the students around them cackled.

He's not worth it, Andy thought. He turned around and continued his way to the parking lot.

"That's right, don't say anything. Just go home and cry to Mommy," Jet said. Andy ignored the comment. *As if.* Jet laughed. "Honestly, I'm not sure who's the bigger loser—Andy Regan or his mom."

Andy's heart pounded. He stopped, then balled his fists and swung around to face Jet. "Don't talk about my mom like that."

Jet crossed his arms. "My mom says she's a loser. Probably because she got to be a lazy housewife up until her husband died on her." Everyone went quiet.

A boy in the crowd took a step forward. "Hey, man. Lay off him a little."

Jet smirked, ignoring the comment. "It'd be hard on me if my son was as lame as you, but being married to a leech like that would definitely kill me." A few of the students gasped.

Andy snarled, lunging for Jet. No one, *no one* talked about his family like that! Jet sauntered sideways, and Andy stumbled to the floor. Jet seized Andy by the collar, raising a fist, and Andy kicked himself for falling into the trap.

"Jet!" said the familiar voice of a girl. "Leave him alone!" Andy scrambled out of Jet's grasp, and looked up to see none other than Zoey Fawsen stomping through the crowd toward them.

Jet let go of Andy, glaring at her. "Aw, Zoey. What's the problem? Is little Andy here your latest boy toy?" He slapped Andy on the back. "I wouldn't do it, bro. I mean, I have no room to talk, since *I* did it, but luckily I didn't catch some sorta disease."

Zoey rolled her eyes, tucking her books under one arm. "What a mature thing to say, Jet. I wish we'd *never* broken up." She bent down and took Andy's hand. "Seriously though, leave him alone, before a teacher shows up and calls the cops or something." Jet's nostrils flared, but he stepped back. Zoey pulled Andy to his feet. "Let's go," she said, and led him toward the school's entrance.

Behind them, students whispered. But Andy was too shocked to care.

They walked out the doors into the senior parking lot, butterflies waging war on Andy's stomach. Hundreds of students laughed and talked under a gray sky. Hundreds more climbed into their cars to drive home. As Andy and Zoey walked past a group of girls in skimpy clothes, the girls stared wide-eyed at them, then huddled together and began whispering.

Zoey shot the girls a quick glare, then gave Andy a sideways glance. "I don't think we've been formally introduced. I'm Zoey Fawsen. What was your name again?"

Andy gulped. "Uh . . . Andrew Regan. Call me Andy." Zoey smiled.

Soon they reached an old red truck, and she dropped his hand, then opened the driver's door. "If that loser made you late for your bus, I can give you a ride home."

Andy bit his thumb. "Oh, that's okay. I'm, uh, parked in the junior lot. That's where I was headed, before he took my phone and . . ."

Andy put his head in his hands, remembering his phone shattering on the commons floor. "Crap. He destroyed my phone. Not sure how I'm going to explain *that* one to my mom."

"Tell her it wasn't your fault. Tell her Jet did it."

Andy shook his head. "No, no. She works for Jet's mom. He's always acted like this toward me, but I usually try to ignore it because I don't want conflict between my mom and her boss. She already has enough on her plate. I'll just have to make something up."

Zoey shrugged. "Whatever works for you, I guess. Want a ride to your car?"

Andy's jaw dropped. "Uh, sure. Thanks." He climbed into the passenger seat, and she started the engine.

When they reached Andy's car in the junior lot, it was sprinkling outside, and most of the students had already cleared out. Only a few couples were left, kissing in the back seats of cars.

Andy's cheeks grew hot. He resisted the urge to bite his thumb. "Hey, uh, Zoey?" She turned toward him. "Thank you. For standing up for me. Sometimes I hear people talking about you." She tensed and looked away, tugging at a curl that framed her face. "But I just want you to know I don't believe anything they say. I think it's all just stupid rumors. You're really cool, and I hope we can be friends."

Zoey smiled but didn't meet his eyes. "I'd like that, Andy. See you around?"

Andy nodded, unbuckling his seat belt. He jumped out of the truck. "See you around."

Lightning flashed in the distance, and Andy waved goodbye as he climbed into his car. He watched her drive away.

Once he reached home, he bolted into his bedroom. He pulled on a sweatshirt, plopped down at his desk, and powered on his computer. The bed was unmade as usual, clothes scattered about the floor. Various cartoon and video game posters were plastered all over the walls. He pulled his headset over his ears and loaded his favorite game's voice chat to tell Mark the exciting news: He'd talked to Zoey. She'd held his hand. She'd even offered to take him home.

The game lit up his monitor with hues of blue and green, and Andy invited Mark to play. Within a few minutes Mark accepted the request, and their characters were thrown into the game.

Andy tapped his fingers on the keyboard. "What's up, dude?" he said into his headset.

"What's up?" Mark replied.

"Jet Weaver annihilated my phone."

"That's rough, buddy."

"Yeah, except *guess* who defended me from him? And held my hand all the way out to the senior parking lot? And offered me a ride home?"

Mark chuckled. "Jennifer Lawrence?"

"No, dumbass. Zoey Fawsen."

"Didn't I tell you not to get involved with that? She's bad news, dude. I heard she, like, slept with a bunch of guys for money when she was a freshman, or somethin' like that."

Andy rolled his eyes. "No way. She's cool. All that stuff everyone says about her—it's wrong." The garage door rumbled open, and Andy ripped off his headset and exited the game. "Sorry, man, gotta go. I'll get on later."

Andy dashed out of his room and down the hallway. He slid onto the hardwood floor of the entryway just as Melissa and his mom opened the door and stepped inside. Melissa squealed in delight, running toward Andy. Her gray eyes glittered, her brown braid flying behind her.

He grinned and scooped her into his arms. "Hey, Mel-Mel. How was your day at school?"

She flung her arms around his neck. "Good. But it would have been better if we weren't doing multiplication." She squirmed out of their embrace and scrambled to the floor. "I hate math."

Andy tugged her braid. "Me too."

Andy's mother winked and tapped his nose. Bits of silver poked through her short, choppy black hair, but her hazel eyes looked more bright and youthful than ever. "I have exciting news." She kicked off her flats and practically skipped into the kitchen, where she set the jeep keys on the counter. "Some things are going to change around here, for the better."

Melissa twirled in place. "What is it?"

Andy raised an eyebrow. "Don't keep us in suspense."

She smiled, bowing dramatically. "Ladies and gentlemen, I hereby present to you the newly hired first-grade teacher of Tumbleweed Elementary." Andy's jaw dropped. "I was a little stressed earlier today because I wasn't sure if I'd gotten the job yet, but now I know for sure—I did. The last several years of school and student teaching have *finally* paid off."

Andy hopped into the kitchen and tackled his mother in a hug. "Mom, that's awesome. I'm so proud of you."

She squeezed him tight. "We're finally going to be a real family. The days of leaving you two home alone while I work or study are over." Melissa joined in on the hug, and for a moment the family stood together, completely engulfed in each other, savoring the moment as if it were a delectable treat.

The excitement didn't last, though. A mournful cry escaped his mom's throat, and she trembled in his arms. He pulled out of their hug and took her hands, looking into her tear-filled eyes. "What's wrong? This is a happy thing."

Her lip quivered. "I just wish your father was—was— I'm sorry. Sometimes it's just hard. Knowing he's not here to see me get this job. To see you two grow up. I mean, I look at the both of you, and I see him. Every day."

Andy nodded. He and Melissa looked almost identical to their dad. They both had his dark-brown hair, his stormy gray eyes, his crooked smile, and his round nose. Sometimes Andy wondered if they inherited any of his mannerisms, but it was hard to remember what his father was like sometimes. He'd tried to preserve the memories, but with each year they grew harder to recall.

Andy pulled his mother and sister into another hug. "Dad said we'd be okay as long as we have each other. And we do. We always will." Andy knew this to be true. No matter what his grades looked like, no matter how much of a weirdo he was, and no matter what Jet said, as long as he had his mom and sister, he'd be okay.

Before anyone could speak another word, the lights of their house went out. The floor erupted in a fit of seizures, and thunder fiercer than a murderous lion roared in the distance.

Zoey sank into the couch in the living room of her and her mother's tiny apartment, scrunching her nose and tugging at a strand of her hair. Her thoughts drifted to her encounter with Jet and how it'd led to meeting a new friend. Probably her only friend.

Andy Regan . . .

Zoey hadn't had a friend since she was in elementary

school. She'd met little Cynthia Watson in the fifth grade, and they'd spent most days climbing trees, catching insects, and playing fetch and tug-of-war with Zoey's cocker spaniel, Daisy. But then, of course, her parents got divorced. She and her mother moved out of that cozy house in Nebraska and left the state, and Zoey hadn't seen Cynthia Watson, Daisy, or even her own father since. He didn't have the decency to call her, or even answer *her* calls, so eventually she'd given up and had her last name changed to her mother's maiden name. Anything to forget.

She pushed the thoughts out of her mind and opened her midterm report. All A+'s, 4.0 GPA. She pursed her lips, her eyes heavy. More than anything she wanted to take a nap, but between school, homework, and her part-time job flipping burgers, this was the only time she had to apply for scholarships.

Essays covered the coffee table in front of her, hundreds of pages and thousands of words stacked on top of each other, written to convince people why she was worthy of their money, why she needed it, how she would put it to good use. She needed all the help she could get to pay for college. After all, her mother wasn't going to pay jack shit for her, even if she could. Then there was the fact that ninety percent of her paychecks went toward rent and bills, and ten percent of a check earned from working in fast food couldn't cover a college loan.

Zoey snatched a pencil, ready to whip out another paper. She was determined to go to college. She needed to get out of her dump of a city, to escape. Where to, she wasn't sure. As long as it was somewhere no one knew her name, where no one could whisper behind her back about something she did years ago, it didn't matter. She needed boys like Jet Weaver to be a thing of the past. She needed a clean slate.

Maybe then she'd follow her dreams. She'd adopt a big lovable dog, go hiking in the mountains, sail the seas, travel the world. She'd become a surgeon or a counselor or a veterinarian. Once she got rid of the bullshit holding her down, the possibilities were endless.

From outside the apartment complex, her mother yelled, "Zoey, get down here and clean out the damned truck!" Zoey rolled her eyes, tossing her pencil aside. She started for the door. If nothing else, she needed to get away from her mother.

She ripped open the door and stomped down the stairs toward the complex's lawn. Her mother sat under the gazebo, smoking a cigarette as rain drizzled down.

Zoey took a deep breath to calm herself and walked toward the gazebo. "Couldn't you have come inside and asked me? Keep yelling like that, and you'll get the cops called on us again."

Her mother narrowed her eyes, tucking a curl behind her ear and puffing on the cigarette. Zoey sighed, shaking her head, then made her way to the parking lot. She unlocked the truck, opened the passenger door, and tucked her textbooks under an arm.

As Zoey walked back toward the apartment, her mother tossed what was left of the cigarette onto the wet grass and crushed it under her sneaker. "Stop acting like such a stuck-up little priss."

Zoey inhaled sharply. She started up the stairs. "I wasn't aware behaving like a decent human being meant I was a stuck-up little priss. Thanks so much for letting me know."

"You're lucky I even let you live here."

Zoey swung around and shot the woman a scowl. "*You're* lucky *I* let *you* live here, since I pay most of your bills and rent."

A *crack* of thunder sounded through the sky, and the ground began to tremor. Zoey gasped, stumbling back, as something skinny and silver shot from the clouds. It came straight for her mother. Zoey dropped her books and pointed at the object. "Look out!" But it pierced her mother through the chest. Her mother's eyes widened, and she slumped to the ground, clutching her heart.

Zoey scrambled toward her mother, trying to figure out what in the world could have hit her. She grabbed the woman by the shoulders and held her upright before she could fall over. What looked like a bloody arrowhead stuck out from her chest.

Her mother coughed, blood trickling from the corners of her lips. "What's happening?"

Zoey's chest tightened. "I don't know." She knew there was no way she could safely remove the arrow. Ripping it out would just make the damage worse. Her mother needed professional medical attention immediately. They needed to call an ambulance, but she'd left her phone in the apartment.

Another arrow, this one glowing and gold, hurtled toward them. Zoey ducked and shielded her mother, and it sped past their heads, then sank into a patch of mud. She couldn't leave her mother outside while she grabbed the phone, nor could she carry her up the stairs. She scanned the complex's yard, but no one else was outside, and she sure as hell wasn't going to scream for help until someone else came to the rescue.

She shot up, grabbed her mother under the armpits, and dragged her toward the truck. "Don't worry, I'm taking you to the hospital."

When they reached the truck, she pulled her mother into the passenger seat and rested her on her side so as to not aggravate the arrow and wound, then clambered into the driver's seat.

She snatched the keys from her pocket, rammed them into the ignition, and floored it. "Hold on."

She sped out of the parking lot. Racing down the street, she dodged parked cars and flew past stop signs. The rain began to pour, beating on the windshield with angry fists, and she peered up at the clouds and gasped in horror. A sea of gold and silver arrows soared down like a battalion of shimmering soldiers racing into battle.

Was it a terrorist attack? Was an enemy country waging

war on the United States? And if one was, why would it be attacking such a small city in Wyoming, where the population was less than forty thousand? Why not New York or Los Angeles?

As the arrows made it to earth, they shattered windows, pierced buildings, and narrowly missed the truck.

The ground shook again, and the truck's rear end shot up. Zoey screamed, her stomach lurching, and then the tires smashed into the road. She hit the brakes, her breaths shallow. "What the hell is going on?"

The trembling slowed into a light vibration, and Zoey glanced at her mother. She was unconscious, her eyes shut tight, her blood seeping into the beige seats of the truck.

For a moment Zoey wondered what she was doing. After all, her mother wasn't good to her. Her mother wouldn't care if something bad happened to her. So why was she out here, braving these arrows, then driving through what seemed to be an earthquake, for someone who couldn't even bother giving her a stable home? She could just leave her. She could fend for herself and let her mother die.

It would solve most of her problems.

No, she thought. *That's not right.*

Lightning flashed in the distance, arrows coming down as fast as the rain. But Zoey slammed her foot onto the gas pedal.

* ~ * ~ * ~

Andy stumbled backward as the house shook. His mom tumbled into the kitchen. She caught herself on the counter, then fell to her knees. Melissa screamed, jerking across the living room. Family pictures fell off the wall, while tiny cracks split the hardwood floor. The ceiling groaned. Their chandelier crashed against the dining table, bits of shiny crystals spiraling through the air.

Melissa darted for the kitchen, screaming, "Mommy!" and the house lurched, throwing her into the air. Her head slammed against the dining table's edge, and her body went limp. She fell to the floor.

Andy lunged for Melissa. He scooped her into his arms and pulled her close to his chest. A stream of blood flowed freely from a gash on her forehead, her eyes closed. His breath caught in his throat. "Mel-Mel . . ."

His mom grabbed her keys off the counter, then ran toward them. The floor lurched again, but he grounded himself, clenching his teeth. "We have to get out of here." His mom nodded, and they dashed out the door, then hurried into the jeep.

Outside, long wailing sirens came from all directions.

The sky was dark gray, lightning blasting, thunder roaring. Monstrous raindrops poured from the clouds, and the earth shook.

Andy's mom sped toward the hospital, gripping the steering wheel so tightly her knuckles were white. She honked her horn, weaving through unruly traffic.

They reached an intersection, and a giant slab of asphalt shot out of the road. Bits of concrete rained down. Five cars ahead crashed into each other. His mom slammed on the brakes, and they slid across the road before the jeep came to a slippery stop.

"We advise everyone to find shelter," the radio host said. "All across the country, there are reports of arrows shooting through the sky, massive thunderstorms, strange earthquakes, and lightning unlike anything we've ever seen. Authorities are investigating the source of this nationwide freak storm, but many citizens fear it may be the wrath of God."

Something silver glittered outside, catching Andy's eye. He looked over and gasped—an arrow was barreling toward the jeep. He shielded Melissa and screamed as it shattered the window, narrowly missing his head. Chunks of glass bit his skin.

"Andy! Melissa!" his mom cried.

Rain poured into the vehicle and soaked his jeans. He yanked the arrow from the leather seat and tossed it outside. "We're okay."

Outside, people jumped from their cars and into the streets, gold and silver arrows lodged in their flailing limbs like pins in a cushion. Even more arrows sailed from the sky. He squinted, trying to spot where they could be coming from, but all he saw were angry storm clouds.

His mom drove around the car accident, weaving through screaming people. "Get out of the way! We need to get to the hospital!"

Andy pulled Melissa as close as their seat belts would allow, willing her to be okay.

* ~ * ~ * ~

Zoey approached a four-way, and the light blinked yellow. "If you people think I'm stopping for you, go ahead and suck it." It turned red. She sped straight through. A horn honked from beside her.

She looked over just as a white jeep hit her truck, and the sound of metal crashing against metal erupted in her ears. Her temple banged against the window. She pumped the brakes, but the truck spiraled out of control. It spun a few more times, then came to a jarring halt, and her head whipped to the side. She blinked in disbelief, trying to process what had happened.

A throbbing ache inched down her neck and into her back. She groaned, struggling to unbuckle her seat belt, then threw open her door. She squinted into the heavy rain.

She was at the edge of a local restaurant's parking lot, the building a heap of bricks and glass. Bloody arms and legs were tangled in the debris. The earthquake had slowed into light vibrations, and now the arrows came in hundreds rather than thousands, but the cries of terrified people still pierced the air. The blare of sirens made her skull pound. She wondered who hadn't made it out of the restaurant in time.

She looked around the parking lot and found the jeep to her left, turned on its side. The scarlet paint of her truck was scraped against its white exterior like a streak of blood in fresh snow. One of the back doors flew open. A skinny, pale, brown-haired young man with square glasses emerged. He dodged a gold arrow, which then impaled one of the jeep's tires, and stumbled toward her. She narrowed her eyes. Was that . . .

She scrambled onto the pavement, and a puddle of water soaked her shoes. "Andy, I'm so sorry. Are you okay?"

Andy shook his head, his eyes filling with tears. "I don't know. My sister— My mom— Are you okay?"

She shivered. "I think so."

"I just need to get to the hospital. My sister hit her head."

"That's where I was going, too. My mom, she's— Never mind. We have to find help. We have to hurry."

Thunder rumbled. A chill ran through Zoey's spine. The sky had opened into an angry vortex, and the largest, most brilliant gold lightning bolt yet shot from it, straight for them. It illuminated the fast-falling raindrops like millions of miniature lightbulbs. Her heart stopped. In that moment, she knew they were dead.

The bolt struck the pavement of the parking lot and filled the air with cement, metal, and screams.

CHAPTER TWO

EXECUTION

Summer, Year 500 AS

The amphitheater was half the size of a city, with slabs of sloping gray stone curved like a crescent moon, making hundreds of rows filled with gods, demigods, nobles, and aristocrats. They were gathered to watch an execution that night, the execution of a traitor.

Karter, Son of Zeus, stood at the edge of the columned temple in front of the amphitheater, staring wide-eyed at the sprawling dirt floor in its center. His head ached, and his limbs trembled. The scar on the right side of his face throbbed with the memory of old pain. He couldn't stop thinking about the girl he knew would die before his own eyes: Syrena, Daughter of Poseidon.

Spencer, Son of Hades, watched the scene beside Karter. His brown eyes usually sparkled with life, but for the last few days, they'd been dull, red, and puffy. His dark skin grew ashen, and although he was still quite muscular, he looked as if he'd been missing meals. Karter couldn't blame him. He had been, too.

A huge, muscular man in white robes descended from the night sky toward the center of the amphitheater, his silver hair and beard shimmering under the constellations. "Greetings, my loyal followers," Zeus, King of the Gods, boomed in a voice like cracks of thunder. He stepped onto the ground. "Tonight, we come together to eliminate a threat to our peaceful reign."

The audience clapped and cheered, but Karter's heart leapt into his throat. How could Syrena do this to the gods? To him, and to Spencer? They were teammates. An invincible trio. He couldn't imagine their lives without her.

Zeus pulled the zigzag gold Lightning Bolt from his robes and brandished it like a sword. It was massive, too big even for his giant arms, and solid, stronger than steel, with sparks of electricity dancing around it. The sight of it made the audience gasp, and Karter shrank back in fear. The Lightning Bolt was the single most powerful object in the entire world. It was the cause of all thunderstorms, and whoever wielded it ruled over the skies. "Poseidon, Lord of the Seas, deliver your daughter," Zeus said.

From the other side of the temple, Poseidon strode out into the amphitheater. He looked a lot like Zeus, but after thousands of years as a sea god, his skin had developed a blue tinge. He dragged Syrena behind him by the chains around her wrists. Even as a prisoner she was regal and beautiful, her features soft as sea-foam, her dark hair cascading down her back in perfect curls.

The pair reached Zeus's side, and Poseidon slammed the base of his three-pronged trident on the ground. The precious gems encrusted on the handle glittered even in the night. The Trident shook the amphitheater, and the audience let out a collective scream. The Trident was the cause of all earthquakes, and whoever wielded it ruled over the saltwater of the world. The tremor subsided, and Poseidon yanked Syrena in front of Zeus and knocked her to her knees. "Let's get this over with quickly," he said, his voice like angry waves swallowing a beach.

Zeus faced the audience. "Syrena, Daughter of Poseidon, has time and time again broken the rules I set in place for my demigod warriors. She has left Olympus without permission, stolen multiple pegasi and weapons, and tried to fulfill the dreaded prophecy. She was once a trusted servant, but now she is deemed a traitor. And she will die." He turned to Syrena and raised the Lightning Bolt above his head. "It's a shame your mortal life had to end this way. Any last words?"

Syrena glared at him and spat at his feet. "I'm not scared of you like I used to be, Zeus. I see it now. I finally understand. You're nothing without the Lightning Bolt."

Zeus slipped the Bolt back into his robes. He raised his arms. They erupted with sparking electricity, and a new, green lightning bolt solidified in his hands. "Death awaits you, and still, you do not cower." Karter held his breath.

"I'm not afraid of death anymore," she said.

Zeus sneered and raised the green bolt. "That is where you are mistaken."

Spencer bolted into the amphitheater. "Wait, *stop*! Don't do this!" He collapsed at Zeus's feet, and the crowd exploded with whispers. "Don't kill her."

Every muscle in Karter's body tensed like a tightly drawn bow. Why would Spencer defy Zeus? He knew the consequences. Karter balled his fists, unable to save either of his friends.

Syrena clutched her heart, her chains clanking. "Spencer, no."

Spencer's eyes filled with tears. "Please, Zeus. I beg you. I love her. I want nothing more than to be with her for all time."

Zeus pointed the green bolt at Spencer's nose. "She has committed unforgivable crimes against the gods. The punishment is death."

Spencer tugged on Zeus's robes. "No—no— please . . ."

Zeus turned toward the temple. He locked eyes with Karter. "Restrain him, my son."

A flicker of hope lit in Karter's heart. It was too late to save Syrena, but perhaps Zeus planned to spare Spencer. He leapt into the air and flew toward Spencer, then seized him. He dragged Spencer across the ground, away from Syrena, and Spencer kicked and thrashed in protest, screaming her name. Karter's eyes filled with tears. "Stop," he said. "It's no use."

Syrena put her face in her hands and wept. Zeus launched the bolt toward her, and it struck her chest in a blast of green light. She screamed and convulsed. The bolt disintegrated, and she fell onto her back, her chest a crater of ash. Her long brown curls fanned out around her head, the smell of smoke and burnt flesh scorching the air.

The crowd cheered, but Karter stared in disbelief at Syrena's lifeless body. Tears rolled down his cheeks. He remembered her laughter on all the days they'd watched sunsets on the beach together. He remembered the way she'd destroyed their enemies with her incredible powers. He remembered the kisses she and Spencer shared as the two danced along the edge of the ocean.

But now her deep-olive skin grew pale, a pained expression etched on her face. Her eyes were wide open, a few last tears trickling down her cheeks.

Spencer squirmed out of Karter's grasp, shaking and crying. "Get off me. Get *off*." He stumbled toward Syrena and fell to his knees beside her.

Zoey's eyes fluttered open. Stars twinkled above her like diamonds against black velvet. She shot up, blood pounding in her ears.

The ground was still, the spicy smell of pine filling her nostrils. The air was heavy, like a humid summer night. There were no screams, no sirens. Only silence.

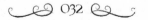

She blinked once, twice, three times, trying to process the scene before her. Where the road had been there were only jagged craters, the sidewalks and parking lots reduced to mangled rubble. Hills of debris lined the edge of where the road once was, where buildings once stood. A few cars were scattered throughout, but they had no tires, no insides. They looked like the rusted shells of what were once automobiles.

Zoey's breaths grew shallow. More terrifying than anything else, there were no people in sight.

From behind her, the familiar voice of a boy said, "Zoey?" She swung around. Even in the dark, she could tell it was Andy, with his youthful face and square glasses.

She scrambled toward him, her heart racing. "Andy! I'm not sure— I don't know what's going on."

Andy sat up and adjusted his glasses. His eyes widened at the scene before him. "Oh my God. The storm—it— it . . ." He climbed to his feet. "Mom! Mel-Mel!" He quickly searched the debris surrounding them and, after finding no one, turned to Zoey with fear in his eyes. "Where is everybody?"

Chills charged through her. If everyone was dead, wouldn't there be bodies? But if everyone was alive, why had they left Andy and her there? It didn't make sense. Her stomach churned. She turned away and threw up, the sour vomit burning her throat.

Andy ran to her and rested a hand on her shoulder. "Are you okay?"

Zoey gasped for breath, holding back tears. "N-no." She wiped her mouth with the sleeve of her flannel. "Something isn't right. This doesn't make sense."

Andy squeezed her shoulder. "It'll be okay. We'll find your mom. We'll find her, and my mom and sister."

Zoey gulped. "Do you have any idea what's going on?"

He shook his head. "All I know is there was a crazy storm. Let's just try to find someone else. Maybe then we'll get some answers." Zoey agreed and climbed to her feet.

For a while they stumbled through the wreckage, searching for any sign of human life. Finally, they found a girl who had to be around eighteen, give or take a year.

The girl was unconscious, sprawled out over debris, her breathing labored. She had to be close to five feet and a hundred pounds soaking wet, with wavy yellow hair that reached her shoulders. Freckles covered her pale skin, and she wore a simple knee-length dress the shade of lush grass. She was like a perfect little pixie.

Andy knelt beside her and poked her arm. "I've never seen her around town. Hello? Are you okay?" Zoey eyed the surrounding wreckage. *So we aren't alone.*

About ten feet ahead of the pixie girl lay a huge sack with oddly shaped utensils hiding in the fabric. Zoey raised an eyebrow and stepped toward the bag. She opened it, then gasped at what she found.

Weapons.

A sword, an axe, several daggers, and four shields were stuffed into the bag, the intricate swirls carved into their iron shining under the moon. She pulled the axe from the bag, stripped the blade of its leather cover, and balanced it in her hands as though she'd held it a million times over.

Andy made his way to her side. He pulled the sword from the bag, his expression that of complete wonder. "No friggin' way. This looks like it came straight out of a gladiator movie." Zoey held the axe up to the sky, admiring the gleaming iron blade.

A head-splitting squawk pierced the silence, breaking Zoey from her trance. In the shadows before them, the strangest creature she'd ever seen glared at them, its eyes glowing green. Its body was that of a giant bird, but its face looked like an old woman's. Long gray hair framed its face.

The bird woman flapped her wings. "Humans. Always so stupid. Always sticking their noses in other people's business." Zoey froze. "I will feast on your flesh!" The bird woman lunged for them, and Zoey screamed, swinging the axe.

The bird woman screeched. She fell back and crashed into the debris, a bleeding gash in her side. Zoey and Andy shared a look of shock, then turned to the monster, grasping their weapons. "Leave us alone," Andy said, his voice shaking.

The bird woman cackled and licked her lips. "I have come back for the Daughter of Apollo. Give her to me, and I will consider sparing you."

Zoey furrowed her brow. *Daughter of Apollo?* She

glanced back at the pixie girl.

"What the hell are you talking about?" Andy said. "You mean the Greek god? Greek gods aren't real."

The bird woman grinned, baring all four of her rotten brown teeth. "Stupid, stupid mortal. You will die first." She leapt at Andy and knocked him onto his back. His sword clattered to the side. Zoey snarled and bolted toward them without a second thought, using all her might to swing the axe at the bird woman's side. The blade cut deep. The bird woman threw her head back and screamed.

Zoey recoiled, sticky blood squirting her cheeks. Andy snatched the sword and scrambled to his feet, then thrust it into the bird woman's chest with a sickening *slice*. He ripped it out and stumbled back. The bird woman coughed and choked, blood trickling down her chin, then fell onto her side and went completely still.

Zoey gasped for breath, looking to Andy with wide eyes. He stared back at her in horror. "What the hell *was* that?" he said.

* ~ * ~ * ~

While the crowd in the amphitheater cheered and clapped, Zeus ordered Karter to drag Spencer back to the temple. Karter did as he was told, and when they made it inside, Zeus grabbed Spencer by the collar of his robes and shook him, his eyes blazing with fury. "I should kill you for your insolence, Son of Hades," Zeus said. "You were not to try and save her." Karter winced. Tears ran down Spencer's cheeks. "Are you listening to me? Have you forgotten your purpose? Your sole purpose in life is to serve *me*. You are a warrior of the gods."

Spencer glared at the ceiling, and Zeus shoved him to the floor. He shook, crawling to his hands and knees, but Zeus kicked him down. "You have one last chance, Spencer," Zeus said. "One last chance to prove your loyalty. If you fail, I will kill you, just as I did Syrena." Karter held his breath, hoping Spencer would do as he was told.

Zeus paced the floor with balled fists. "My second Harpy has yet to return with the Daughter of Apollo, and I can't help but think she has been slain. Neither of you has ever been on a mission to capture a fellow demigod, but after this disaster, I think it is time. Go with Karter. Find Diana. Catch her, and bring her to me."

Karter took a step toward his father and bowed his head. "We will not fail you, Father. Did the Harpy that returned with Syrena see Diana? Does she have any idea where she may be?"

Zeus nodded. "Far to the west. In the forest. We will extract her memory of the place, and Hermes will make a portal there so you can begin your search. I'll send you with pegasi so you may fly home."

Spencer dropped his head, and a strangled cry escaped his throat. He wiped his eyes, then turned to Zeus. "I will not fail you, my king." Karter sighed in relief.

* ~ * ~ * ~

Zoey shook her head, barely able to process what had just happened.

The city was destroyed. Everyone was gone. They'd had to kill a freaky monster, and that freaky monster said she was coming back for the Daughter of Apollo.

Daughter. Of. Apollo.

Zoey wiped the blood from her face and eyed the pixie girl. Maybe her dad just had eccentric parents who gave him a strange name. But that didn't explain why such a monster had come after her. Zoey didn't believe in gods— she'd always considered herself atheist—but aside from an alien invasion, she couldn't think of a plausible explanation for what was transpiring other than the paranormal.

She grabbed the bag of weapons and shoved it into Andy's hands, then ran to the pixie girl. She grabbed her under the armpits and pulled her through the wreckage. "We need to get out of here," she said. "We need to find a place to hide."

Andy chased after her. "No, wait. We have to stay where we are. How will anyone find us if we leave? Our families are probably looking for us right now."

Zoey frowned. "I'm not sure they're even still alive, Andy. But we are, and to stay that way, we need to hide. I'm not sure what that *thing* was, but what if more come after us? I have a feeling we were only able to kill it because this girl already roughed it up a bit."

Andy shook his head. "No. Our families are alive. They can't be dead. They can't be." His voice shook.

Zoey sighed in exasperation. She opened her mouth to speak, but before she could say a word, a flash of purple light sliced through the empty air behind them. A gust of powerful wind sent them tumbling backward, and sharp debris ripped Zoey's jeans, scraping her knees. The purple light rippled and bubbled, growing brighter and brighter as it morphed into an oval shape, and two figures stepped out from it as if it were an open door with nothing on the other side.

Zoey narrowed her eyes. The figures were two young men around twenty years old, seated on white horses with angelic feathered wings. They spotted Zoey and Andy, then hopped off the horses.

The taller one was muscular, over six feet, and wore black robes that fell past his knees. He held a seven-foot-long spear. His skin and curly locks were a deep shade of brown. His attractive, angular facial features were drawn in torment, and his dark eyes were puffy, as though he'd been crying for days.

The other man wore similar burgundy robes over his lean figure. He would have been handsome, with his shaggy black hair, full lips, and striking golden eyes glowing like embers in a campfire, but his skin was so pale it seemed gray, and a scar like the branches of a brittle tree twisted up the right side of his face and neck.

The purple light dissolved into the darkness, and Zoey

detangled her limbs from the pixie girl's. She scrambled to her feet and grabbed the axe. "Who the hell are you?"

Scarface eyed her up and down, then gestured toward the pixie girl at her side. "We're here for the Daughter of Apollo. Hand her over, and we'll do you no harm." His voice was like a snake slithering through dry grass.

Zoey knit her brow, looking back at the girl. She was still unconscious, her breathing labored. "Why is everyone after her?"

Andy grabbed Zoey's arm and pulled her down. "What are you doing?"

Zoey yanked her arm away. "I'm about to figure out what's going on," she snapped, then turned back to the two young men. "So answer my question. Why is everyone after her? What's going on? And who are you?"

Scarface glanced over the scenery, his eyes growing wide when he spotted the dead bird woman. "Who did this? Who killed the Harpy?"

Zoey brandished the axe. "We did."

Scarface rubbed his temples. "Insolent girl. I'm going to tell you one more time, and after this I can't promise what will become of you. Give us the Daughter of Apollo."

Zoey tightened her grip on the axe. "No. Not until I get some answers."

Scarface lunged toward her. He knocked the axe from her hands and seized her wrists with surprising strength. Andy jumped to his feet, sword in hand, but Scarface kicked him in the chest. He flew back and hit his head on a rock, then, with a groan, slipped into unconsciousness.

"Andy!" Zoey cried, her heart in her throat.

Scarface glared down at her. "Don't make me hurt you."

Zoey nodded, the rest of her body paralyzed, and Scarface released her. She fell to her knees. Scarface picked up the pixie girl in one swift movement, then threw her over his shoulder. He swung around to face his more attractive friend, but sucked in a sharp breath as he was met with the tip of the seven-foot spear at his throat.

A tear trickled down his friend's cheek, his breaths shallow. "Put her down, Karter. Put Diana down." His voice was deep and gloomy.

Karter gulped. "Spencer, don't do this. Zeus himself demanded we bring her into custody."

Spencer pressed the spear against Karter's neck. "Whatever Syrena and Diana did, it must have worked." He jerked his head in Zoey and Andy's direction. "Those mortals don't seem to know what's going on. What if they're part of the prophecy? Put Diana down. *Now.*" Karter let Diana fall.

Zoey wanted to run away. She wanted to escape, to protect herself. But she couldn't leave Andy or Diana. Andy was the closest thing she had to a friend, and she couldn't begin to imagine what would become of Diana if these crazy people got ahold of her. She grabbed Diana and the axe, then dragged them toward Andy so she could protect them. If she died trying, so be it.

Spencer pulled the spear against his side, and the two began to circle each other. "I'm a traitor now," Spencer said. "Why don't you go ahead and fight me?"

Karter's lip quivered. "You're my best friend. I don't want to fight you. I want you to do what is asked of you, so you can live."

Spencer paused, chuckling. "Syrena was your best friend too. And yet you didn't do anything to try and save her. If you don't care about her, you don't care about me."

Karter snarled, raising an arm. Sparks of electricity erupted from his chest, then snaked up his arm and into his palm. A zigzag golden lightning bolt solidified in his hand, and he launched it at Spencer's feet. Spencer dodged the attack. The bolt struck the debris, shaking the ground. The winged horses' eyes went wide, and they neighed, rearing on their hind legs.

Spencer's nostrils flared. "I hate you." He threw his spear aside and pounded his fists into the wreckage. The earth trembled from the impact, a sound like thousands of lost souls wailing ringing in Zoey's ears. Dust swirled up from the debris and surrounded Spencer like a sandstorm.

The dust began to take form: skulls, femurs, ribcages. Hundreds of bones solidified around him, bobbing up and down in a terrifying dance of death. Then they came together, cracking into place, forming an army of five skeletal soldiers moaning and groaning like a horde of bloodthirsty zombies.

The winged horses flapped their wings, but before they could escape, Spencer grabbed them by the reins. He looked to the skeletons. "My soldiers, go! After Karter!"

Karter's eyes widened. He leapt into the air and, although he had no wings, flew into the sky as if it were as simple as riding a bike. The army of skeletons marched through the debris after him. Soon enough, they all disappeared into the night.

Zoey was petrified. Her mind raced, trying to process what just happened, but it felt like a nightmare, like at any moment she'd wake up cocooned by bed-sheets and gasping in horror.

Once Spencer calmed the winged horses, he turned to her. She shuddered at the sight of him, only able to think of skeletons and spears. "Hey, it's okay," he said, his tone gentle. "There's nothing to be afraid of now. I'm not going to hurt you. And when those two wake up, we'll figure out exactly what's going on."

CHAPTER THREE

APOCALYPSE

For what felt like a painful eternity, Karter flew high above the pine trees of the forest, stars shimmering against the night sky. The small army of skeletons moaned as they trekked below him.

It wasn't that he didn't know how to kill them; all he had to do was destroy their skulls. But doing so would make the night's events real. Facing Spencer's army head-on and killing them outside of training would prove all of it wasn't just an awful dream.

Karter gasped for breath, struggling to keep himself in the air. His body was heavy, a familiar burning sensation erupting in his chest. He clutched his heart. He'd used a lot of power. Holding Spencer down, the lightning, the hours of flying—he'd sapped his strength. If he didn't stop soon, he could weaken himself and succumb to the skeletons.

It was time to face reality. He couldn't keep running— he had to kill them.

He swooped down and kicked two of their skulls, and

chunks of bone flew through the air. Three more advanced on him, grinding their teeth, reaching for him with bony hands. He channeled his strength and seized two by their necks, then slammed their heads together. With a loud *crunch*, their skulls shattered. They slumped to the ground.

There was just one left.

The final skeleton snarled, leaping toward him. He focused his power and jumped high into the air, then balled a fist and sent his knuckles straight through its head.

Exhausted, Karter shuffled through the trees afterward, trying to catch his breath, his limbs as weak and wobbly as overcooked noodles. Eventually he found a stream and collapsed beside it.

He glared into the fast-moving water, at his hideous reflection, his golden irises glowing in the night. He wished they were still brown. The gold drew even more unnecessary attention to his face.

Syrena's death and Spencer's act of treason played through his head like a tragic song. He wondered if he should go home and tell his father what happened, or if he should go after Spencer. He could try to convince Spencer to take back what he'd done, to admit what a huge mistake he'd made; then maybe Spencer would help capture Diana.

One thing was for sure. If he could avoid telling his father, he would. If his father found out, he'd kill Spencer for sure. He'd punish Karter . . .

There had to be another way.

A shooting star sailed through the dark sky, and he

closed his eyes. "If there's a single god out there willing to help me, please, give me your wisdom."

A woman's voice said, "Greetings, Son of Zeus."

Karter almost wet his robes. He swung around, tripped over himself, and splashed into the stream. Before him stood a beautiful pale woman with curly red hair that fell just past her shoulders. Her eyes were silver and glittered like moonlight on a lake. Although the tunic she wore was pitch-black, the fabric shimmered with constellations and shooting stars.

He hoisted himself up, cold water dripping off his body. "Who are you?"

She smiled and curtsied. "I am Asteria. Titan goddess of stars, prophetic dreams, and necromancy."

"Titan?" He backed away. He'd always been taught to mistrust Titans.

Asteria frowned. "Yes, I am a Titan goddess. But I mean you no harm."

He gritted his teeth. "Go away."

She sighed. "You asked for guidance, Karter, and I answered your prayer. Now would you like my help? Or shall I, the only god answering your plea, return to my island? I would be much safer there. Your father would have no chance of hurting me if I stayed hidden."

He narrowed his eyes. "What do you mean, he wouldn't have a chance to hurt you? My father is a great and fair king."

Asteria smiled and shook her head. "You have much

to learn." Before he could respond, she disintegrated into millions of miniature glittering stars.

~~*~

Andy awoke lying on his back. He groaned, his head aching. He sat up and rubbed the bump on the back of his skull. The rising sun cast rays over the wreckage of his town, which glared into his glasses and made his eyes water.

There was a blur of movement in front of him, of curly brown hair and sky-blue eyes. A pair of arms wrapped him in a tight embrace. "Andy!" Zoey cried. "You're awake."

He hugged Zoey's shoulders. It was all coming back to him now: a scar-faced creep had attacked her, and when Andy tried to step in, the creep knocked him aside. "Thank God you're okay," he said, then buried his face in her shoulder, his cheeks growing hot.

Zoey pulled out of their hug, and another girl approached them. She was tiny, with bright green eyes, blonde hair, and pale, freckled skin. The "Daughter of Apollo."

She knelt in front of him and pressed her palm against his forehead. "Zoey told us your name is Andy. You have a head injury." Her voice was melodious, like an airy tune played on a flute. "I'm sorry I waited this long to heal you, but I'm not sure you'd believe what we have to tell you if I'd done it while you were out."

Andy furrowed his brow, unsure of what she meant,

but then her hand lit up with brilliant light, and he shut his eyes. Warm, tingling energy radiated from her palm, flooding his skull and trickling through every last inch of his body, and his headache diminished. It was the strangest sensation he'd ever experienced.

The warmth subsided, and Andy's eyes fluttered open. Zoey, the freckled girl, and the gloomy young man with the spear sat before him. Two white winged horses were tied to the rusted shell of a car a short walk away.

Andy adjusted his glasses and raised an eyebrow at the young man, then pointed at the freckled girl. "Wait, what? Weren't you just trying to capture her? And what's with the winged horses? This is freakin' me out."

She pulled her hand from Andy's forehead. "Those aren't horses. They're pegasi. And Spencer was trying to capture me, but he's on our side now."

"Pegasi? Is that plural, like for Pegasus?" Diana nodded. "Ohhh-kayyy," Andy said, confused. "I guess, uh, thank you. For, uh, fixing me? How did you do that?"

She smirked, her eyes sparkling with mischief. "It's one of my powers."

Andy shot Zoey a disbelieving glance, but she only shrugged, seemingly unfazed by the girl's answer. "A power, all right," he said, and turned back to the freckled girl. "So, what's going on? Who are you guys? There was a storm—with arrows, earthquakes, and then this crazy lightning bolt—and then there was this bird-monster thing. What's that all about? I need to know so I can find my family. They're probably freaking out trying to find me right now."

The girl gave him a hard look. "My name is Diana. Like I said before, he's Spencer. As for what's going on—well, the simplest way I could put it is that the storm was the end of the world."

Andy chuckled. "The end of the world? You're kidding, right?" Diana shook her head, and Spencer stared at him with serious eyes as dark as the deepest pits of hell.

Okay, apparently they were serious. And probably experiencing a psychotic break from the trauma of the storm.

Andy turned to Zoey. Her cheeks were pale. "You don't seriously believe them, do you?" he said.

Her lip quivered. "I don't know. I don't know what to believe. Was the storm some kind of alien invasion?"

Spencer cleared his throat. "Not aliens, but gods. Greek gods."

Andy narrowed his eyes. "But Greek gods aren't real. What about God? You know, *the* God? The guy in charge of everything?"

Spencer shrugged. "If he does exist, he doesn't interfere with what the gods have done."

Zoey balled her fists. "This doesn't make sense. Gods aren't real. I don't understand."

Spencer rose. He made his way to Andy and Zoey and knelt in front of them. "I am a demigod Son of Hades, King of the Underworld, and if you'll let me, I can show you what we say is true." He pressed his thumbs between their eyes, and in a swirl of fog, Andy was swept away.

~~*~

Screaming. It surrounded Karter, deafening and spine tingling. It was Syrena. She needed him.

It was dark, so dark he couldn't even see his hands in front of his face. But he ran anyway. Ran until his breaths were shallow. His legs numb. His throat burning.

"Karter!" Syrena screamed. "Help me!"

Then he saw her. A ray of white light shone down on her, and she struggled against iron chains bolted to the ground, shackled around her wrists and ankles. Her hair was stuck to her face with sweat. Tears streamed down her cheeks. "Please, my friend, save me," she said, her voice hoarse.

He ran to her and seized the chains. He tried to pry them apart, but even his gift of strength wasn't enough to bend the metal. "I can't." He fell back. "I can't do it. I'm not strong enough."

A disembodied laugh pierced the air, deep and booming and sinister, a laugh that sounded much like his father. "You are stronger than you think. An important pawn of the game."

A surge of familiar, hot power coursed through Karter's veins and shot down his arm. His hand sparked with electricity, and a green bolt solidified in it, hissing with as much power as his father's Lightning Bolt. "Green lightning," he said, unable to believe he held it in his hands. "But I've never . . ." His arm raised itself and aimed the bolt directly at Syrena. He struggled against it. "No!" he cried, as he involuntarily launched the bolt at her chest. She screamed.

He fell to his knees, his body weak, his mind numb. She convulsed, and the lightning sucked the life from her body until her eyes went dull. She fell slack, her chains clanking against the ground.

His father's cackle echoed behind him, and the strangely familiar voice of a woman said, "Spencer goes west."

Karter's eyes fluttered open, his body tense and drenched in sweat.

He'd killed Syrena—

He'd killed her—

No, wait—

Zeus killed her.

Karter looked around, finding he'd drifted to sleep in the forest near the stream. He wondered if any monsters had seen him, and shuddered at the thought of being attacked in his sleep. At least now that he'd slept he felt rejuvenated. All the strength he'd lost rushed back into his body like liquid gold coursing through his veins.

He stood, rays of sunlight peeking through the pine trees. He couldn't go home without Spencer on his side and Diana in custody. He couldn't lose Spencer like he'd lost Syrena.

Spencer goes west.

He turned toward where he'd come from, starting his journey back to the ruins of the old city.

* ~ * ~ * ~

The fog cleared, and Andy screamed, barreling through a black abyss, the sounds of horns honking and tires screeching reverberating in the darkness.

He felt as if his body were being sucked through a straw. He jolted upward, suddenly in the passenger seat of his mother's jeep. It was exactly like the scene only a day prior, but colorless, and cloudy around the edges.

Andy's chest twisted into a panicked knot. His mother was weaving through heavy traffic, clutching the steering wheel with white knuckles. He spun around, and gasped when he saw himself in the back seat of the car, cradling his unconscious and bleeding sister as best as he could despite their seat belts.

He reached for his mother. He reached for his sister. He screamed for them, but as he touched them, his hands went through their bodies, like a ghost going through a wall.

What was going on? What was Spencer doing to him?

The sound of metal crashing against metal erupted in his ears. He tumbled from his seat and flew through the windshield. His mother screamed, "Melissa! Andy!"

The air flickered as if someone were fast-forwarding a video, and suddenly he was hovering over the parking lot. It was just like the day before—they'd hit Zoey's truck.

Everything around him slowed. The sound of sirens, the screaming people, even the rain. Light flashed through the sky, and he looked up, a lightning bolt coming straight for him. He closed his eyes and braced for the pain that was sure to come.

But he felt nothing.

He was jolted into the sky by an unknown force. He tried to look back, to see his mother and sister, but only caught a glimpse of a slow-motion explosion. Of billowing smoke, of concrete chunks, of flailing limbs.

He reached a cluster of storm clouds and came to a jarring halt. Before him, a giant of a man floated above the clouds. He held a lightning bolt in his burly hands, his face full of fury. "We will rule the world once again." He launched the bolt at the earth, and after a spine-chilling *crack* of thunder, Andy jolted higher into the sky.

As he ascended, more figures materialized. A young man and a young woman, shooting arrow after arrow toward earth. Then a bearded man with a three-pronged trident, and as he flicked his wrists, visions of oceans overtaking whole cities and earthquakes bringing down skyscrapers flashed across Andy's eyes.

In that moment, Andy knew in his gut that he was seeing visions of the day before.

Diana and Spencer were telling the truth.

Fog crept into the corners of his vision and swallowed him whole.

Within a minute or so the fog faded away. He gasped for breath, digging his nails into the ground as his vision cleared. He was back in the ruins of his town.

Zoey sat beside him, clutching her knees. Diana and Spencer kneeled in front of them, and Spencer panted, sweat rolling down his forehead.

Zoey bit her lip. "All right. I believe you. The Greek gods are real; the storm was the end of the world. But how—how did you do that?"

Spencer wiped his face. "It's one of my powers. If a moment in time is saturated with death, I can channel visions of it into my mind, and the minds of others. Because so many died during the Storm, I was able to give you a clear vision of how it happened."

Andy's jaw fell. *A moment saturated with death* . . . "Okay, whatever. So Greek gods are real. I don't care. Where's my family? My mom and sister? The rest of the people in our town? Give me a straight answer, or I'll go find them myself."

Diana rested a gentle hand on his arm. "Andy, there's not a good way to say this." He held his breath, afraid he already knew what was coming. "So, I'll just come out and say it. Your family is dead. Everyone in your town is dead."

Andy shoved her away. He stood up, only to stumble backward, shivers racking his body. "No. You're lying."

Diana sighed, her eyes solemn. "Only a few hundred thousand people in this country lived through the Storm. No one in your town survived, not even you and Zoey. After I woke up, Spencer and I asked Zoey a few questions, then discussed all this privately, and we came to the conclusion that you two must be the fulfillment of a prophecy. Because of my friend, because she sacrificed her life, you were born again, and brought forward in time."

Zoey clutched her chest. "Brought forward in time?"

Spencer nodded. "The vision I gave you happened five hundred years ago. You're in the year 500 AS—After Storm."

Zoey's gaze fell to the ground. "But how—how could she have done that? How is that even possible?"

Andy's eyes filled with tears. He didn't care what year they were in. He didn't care if he'd died and been brought back to life. He didn't care about anything but the fact that once again, God or the universe or whoever the hell was in charge up there had wronged him.

He hugged his sides and gasped for air. The world around him closed in like a dark, shrinking tunnel. "I don't deserve to be alive. Not when they're dead." Pain shot through his chest like a bullet through his heart, sobs escaping his body in violent shudders. A familiar emptiness drowned everything and everyone around him; excruciating pain consumed him. The same pain he'd felt when his father died.

He turned around and dashed away.

"Andy!" Zoey called from behind. "Stop!"

But he didn't stop. Instead he ran faster, his feet pounding against jagged debris. At the edge of the ruins, a forest of pine trees lined across rolling hills beckoned him, bushes and wildflowers swaying in the breeze. Rays of cheery sunlight shone on it from behind him, and he shook his head in disbelief at the sight. There had never been so many trees outside his town. So many hills, so many flowers. Only a day ago it had been dry grassland and lots of dirt. *There has to be some kind of mistake. Please let it be a mistake.*

Memories of his father's death flooded back, as if the comfort of his remaining family had kept him together for the last four years. He remembered the white walls of the hospital room, the yells of nurses, the sickening smell of death. The flowers with cards saying "sorry for your loss" that didn't help at all, even if the people who sent them meant well. The black casket as they lowered it into the grave.

And what happened to his mother's body? To Mark's? To Mel-Mel's? They wouldn't have gotten funerals. If everyone in his city died, and he and Zoey were really five hundred years into the future, what had become of all those bodies? Had they been left out in the open? He imagined their mangled corpses rotting in the sun. He smelled it, the putrid stench of decaying flesh.

One question rose above all others, numbing him like a doctor injecting every square inch of his body with local anesthesia. Why was God—the universe—whoever was in charge—punishing him like this? Why couldn't he have stayed dead with everyone else?

He felt as though he'd been running for hours, finally reaching the shade of the trees. His sneakers sank into spongy earth with every step. Behind him, Zoey cried his name, telling him to "come back" and "be rational about all this," but how was he supposed to be rational? All of it was crazy. It didn't deserve rationality, and he didn't want to go back. He wanted to run, wanted to be alone. He wanted to die.

He darted through the trees, up and down hills, twisting and turning until all he could see was forest, his town left far behind.

After a while he had to pause. He clutched his knees and gasped for breath. Sweat rolled off his body, the air sticky and humid. There was a long hiss somewhere ahead, and he raised an eyebrow, eyeing the forest. *What was that?*

As if to answer his thoughts, a creature as strange as the bird woman slithered through the trees toward him, knocking a few down in its path.

It was like an anaconda, probably thirty feet long and wide enough to stomach a cow. It had two snake heads, one on either end of its body. Its scales glittered like dark sapphires, its beady eyes the color of blood.

Andy held his breath and froze. Maybe if he didn't move, it wouldn't see him?

The creature cocked its heads and looked him up and down, then threw both back and let out a guttural scream that shook the trees, baring two sets of yellow fangs dripping with gooey saliva.

Andy's instincts told him to run. Told him to find Diana and Spencer, told him to live.

But deep down he didn't want to live.

So he stood there, heart in his throat as the creature advanced, ready for his inevitable death.

CHAPTER FOUR

PROPHECY

Zoey's gut clenched when up ahead, a scream sounded and the trees began to shake. "Andy's in trouble," she said, looking back at Spencer as he ran behind her.

Above the trees, Diana flew on one of the pegasi. The other flapped its wings beside them. She pulled an arrow from the pack on her back and drew her bow. "I wonder what gave you that idea," she yelled, then kicked the pegasus's sides and sped toward the screams. Zoey and Spencer followed close behind.

Within a few moments, they reached a forest clearing that looked as though multiple trees had been knocked down. A blue serpentine monster with a head on each end of its body had Andy hanging limp from one of its mouths.

When it saw them it screamed, the trees shaking, and let Andy fall onto his back. He hugged his leg and let out a weak cry.

Diana landed and tied both pegasi to a tree. "It's the

Amphisbaena," she said. The pegasi reared up on their hind legs as if in panic. "Don't worry, you two. I won't let it get you." She turned around and sent an arrow straight into one of the monster's blood-red eyes. It recoiled, screaming.

The Amphisbaena jerked one head at her and snapped its jaws, but she leapt out of the way like a ballerina. Mid-air, she shot an arrow into the same head's other eye. It screamed again and fell back, then let the unharmed head take charge.

Zoey looked to Spencer, clutching the axe she'd used earlier. "What do you want me to do?"

Spencer narrowed his eyes at the monster and waved his spear. "Get Andy out of the way. We'll take care of this." He bolted toward the monster, jumped onto its middle, then stabbed it repeatedly. Diana sent more arrows toward its heads.

Zoey kept her head low, trying to stay out of the Amphisbaena's sight as she ran to Andy. She reached him, a hole in his thigh gushing with blood, so deep she could see his bone. His face was even paler than usual. His skin was hot and sticky to the touch, and he let out a moan when he saw her. "Z-Zoey."

She shushed him, then grabbed him under the armpits and dragged him away from the Amphisbaena, trying to hold back her tears.

They reached a cluster of trees, and Zoey rested his head against a patch of grass. "What were you thinking?"

she said.

He coughed and trembled. "It's t-too m-much. A-all of it."

Zoey understood what he meant. At face value, everything they'd been told sounded crazy. But somewhere deep in her gut, she knew it was all real, even if she had an infinite number of questions left to ask. She'd seen winged horses and bird women. She'd seen Diana heal with warm gold light, Karter shoot lightning from his hands and fly, and Spencer summon skeletons. She'd witnessed a vision that perfectly explained the strange storm—the lightning, the earthquakes, the arrows.

On top of all that, she *wanted* it to be real. She'd always wished for a clean slate, a place where she'd never again have to face the judgment of others for her bad decisions. She'd never have to flip another burger again, she'd never have to see her insufferable classmates again, she'd never have to see her mother again, and best of all, her father was dead now, so she wouldn't have to keep hoping he'd get in contact with her.

Sure, going to college, pursuing a good career, adopting a dog, and traveling the world was out of the question. But did that really matter as long as she'd escaped her life from before? Losing those things didn't mean she had no purpose. Diana and Spencer had mentioned a prophecy and said she and Andy must be a part of it. That had to be important, right?

Thinking about it made her heart heavy with guilt, but

that didn't change the truth. She was happy to be there—scared, but happy.

She took Andy's hands and squeezed them tight. "There's a reason we're here, Andy. Don't you want to find out what it is?" The Amphisbaena screamed again, and Zoey furrowed her brow, peering between branches.

Diana shot her last arrow, which pierced the monster's stomach, while Spencer launched his spear into its throat. It slithered back toward the trees as if in retreat, weapons lodged all over its body, but Diana tossed her bow aside and raised her hands to the sky. In them an orb of gold light began to grow, like a miniature sun blazing in her palms.

Diana smirked. "No way I'd let you get away that easy." She chucked the sphere of light, and it flew through the air like a ball perfectly served in a game. It hit one of the Amphisbaena's heads with explosive force, chunks of thick skull and slimy brains splattering all over the ground. The remaining head screamed in agony, its twin a bloody stump, and Diana conjured another sphere of light, then blasted the head into oblivion.

Zoey's jaw dropped. She had a million questions, eager to discover how all the powers worked.

Her excitement faded as Andy let out a whimper. Blood trickled from his mouth and down his chin. "Diana! Spencer!" she cried. "Andy needs your help. I think—I think he's dying!"

Diana and Spencer rushed to them, and Diana took

Andy in her arms. Her hands glowed with gold light as she healed him. "Don't you *dare* run away again," she said. "You can't die. You're too important. You both are."

Andy groaned, his body lighting up with hers. "The storm really was the end of the world, wasn't it?"

Spencer nodded. "The Greek gods, the ones you were told were myths—well, they're real. Diana and I are their children. We're demigods: half human, half god. We're not immortal—we'll die one day, just like you, even though we have some divine blood. Diana is the Daughter of Apollo, god of sunlight, healing, archery, music, art, oracles, and poetry."

Andy grunted. "That's a lot to be in charge of."

"And I'm the Son of Hades. He's the god of riches, the dead, and the underworld."

"I bet you're *great* at Halloween parties," Andy said.

Spencer cleared his throat. "As you saw in the vision I gave you, the gods destroyed the modern world. It was out of anger at humanity. After hundreds of years, their stories became nothing more than myth. Some minor gods even began to fade away. And when that happened—well, everyone else got scared. A god's greatest fear is to fade away completely. They'd had enough. Apollo and his twin sister, Artemis, filled the sky with their arrows. Poseidon shook the earth and swallowed the coasts. Zeus made a storm, with lightning that struck every town, every city, every state. And when they were done, that wasn't the end of it."

The light faded from Diana's hands, and she pulled away from Andy, sweat rolling down her forehead. The color returned to Andy's cheeks, his wounds gone. "Hades opened the ground of the countries' graveyards and brought a new, evil life to all the corpses," Diana said. "They terrorized anyone who defied the gods until the elements wore their bodies away. Demeter sucked the life out of the crops, made the soil so terrible no one could grow anything for many years, and a lot of people starved to death. Ares convinced numerous countries to declare war, causing mass destruction."

"Are there any people left?" Zoey said. "Any regular people, like us? Not demigods?"

"Of course," Diana said. "The whole point of ruling the world was to have worshippers. Without worshippers, eventually even the most well-known gods would die off. In this country, there are twelve cities near the east coast, where many of the gods' loyal worshippers live in comfort. They're descendants of humans who begged for mercy, who bowed down. Each of the twelve cities honors one of the twelve Olympians: the most prominent deities of the Greek pantheon."

"And what happened to the rest of the world?" Zoey asked.

"The rest of the gods and goddesses have cities full of worshippers all across the globe," Diana replied.

Andy sat up. "So all the people left are just mindless sheep?"

Spencer shook his head. "No. In the last few years, groups of people rioted in the streets of the cities and were killed. There are also small, scattered villages, where people who refuse to worship the gods live. But they struggle to survive, and many are picked off by monsters."

"Monsters," Zoey said. "Like the one you guys just killed. The Amphisbaena. Did the gods create them? I mean, monsters didn't exist as far as I knew."

Diana sighed. "Monsters were alive in the old days, but were killed off by demigods and heroes, and as time went on, people came to the conclusion that they had just never existed. But after the world ended, the gods brought all the monsters back to life to scare people into submission. The Amphisbaena was originally born in the deserts of Libya, when Perseus flew over it carrying the head of Medusa. Her gorgon blood dripped onto the sand, and the Amphisbaena was born."

Andy put his hands up. "Okay, slow down. If Zoey and I are so important, we need to know a few things. First off, how did we get here? And why are we here? Why aren't we still dead, like everyone else? How does that even work?"

Diana shrugged. "I don't know the answers to all of those questions just yet, but before Syrena and I went through with our plan to bring you here, we asked the three deities called the Fates to give us answers. They didn't tell us much, but they said they'd reveal more once we succeeded in bringing you here. All I really know is you're the fulfillment of a prophecy, one that determines the fate of the world and the future of humanity."

Zoey gasped, her heart in her throat. "Fate of the world? Future of humanity?"

Diana nodded, her eyes serious. "You two are here to fight, and hopefully defeat, the gods."

Zoey had known she was there for a reason, but she hadn't thought it was so drastic. "You really mean *we're* expected to save the world?" She wasn't sure she was capable of becoming an apocalyptic superhero. Maybe a sidekick? Those guys were pretty important.

Andy narrowed his eyes. "A world we don't even know. A world where our families and friends have been long dead. Isn't there a way to go back to our own time and stop all this from happening in the first place?"

Diana frowned. "No."

Andy scowled, climbing to his feet. "This is stupid. I just want to go home."

Spencer and Diana tensed, and Zoey shot him a glare. "At least we're alive," she said.

Andy let out a cold laugh. "What do you think happens to us if we fail at what they're asking us to do? Which, by the way, is more than likely. Think about it—we're being asked to fight gods. Gods, Zoey. No matter what we choose to do, we're dead."

Zoey rolled her eyes. "Way to stay positive." She turned to Diana and Spencer. "All right, you said we're part of a prophecy. But what does the prophecy say exactly? Does it say we'll win the fight?"

Diana pressed her lips into a thin line. "It doesn't say you'll beat them. It's pretty vague, to be honest."

"Then what the hell *does* it say?" Andy said.

Diana sighed, wringing her hands. "It says, *When the world is taken back, and monsters rule the trees, blood of a demigod will spill. Two mortals will rise, two from the Before, reborn from sacrifice. And when the sky is black and green, and the heavens cry, they will lead a war. A war on the gods.*"

Andy shot Zoey a triumphant glare. "Okay, so it said we'd be leading a war. But it said *nothing* about winning the war. I rest my case. We're dead."

"If you weren't a threat, the war wouldn't have been foretold in the first place," Diana said. "Don't rule out your victory."

"But you're asking us to achieve the impossible," Andy said.

"It's not impossible," Diana snapped, climbing to her feet. "The Fates told Syrena and me that it could happen, and that they'd disclose to you and Zoey how to do it once you were here."

Andy balled his fists. "I'm not doing this. Not any of it. It's crazy."

Zoey took a deep breath. If Spencer and Diana really thought there was a way to win a war on the gods, maybe they could do it. "I get that you're upset. We've lost our lives from the past. But it sounds like the world needs us. Maybe we can do this. Maybe we can bring peace and—"

"No," Andy growled, shaking his fists. He swung

around and stomped farther into the trees.

Zoey jumped to her feet and chased after him. "Andy, stop," she said, seizing his arm. "Please. There's nothing else we can do. There's no way to go back to our old lives." She traced her hand down his arm and laced her fingers with his. He glanced over his shoulder at her, and his gaze softened. "The gods are the ones who killed our families. And if there's a chance we can defeat them, to save humanity, don't you want to try? I do. Please, come with me."

There was a long pause, and Zoey stared hard into Andy's eyes. They were as gray as the fierce waves of a hurricane.

Finally, Andy bit his lip and broke their gaze. "Fine. I'll go with you."

Zoey sighed in relief, pulling Andy into a long, deep hug. The smells of sharp cinnamon and citrus lingered on his tattered hoodie. "Thank you," she whispered into his shoulder, then let go of him. They turned to Diana and Spencer.

Andy hung his head. "So . . . we have to talk to the 'Fates'? Who are they? And *where* are they? How are we going to reach them?"

Diana put her hands on her hips and smirked. "The Fates are the incarnations of destiny, and they control every living being's thread of life. They have the answers to just about anything. To get to them, we're going to fly on the backs of those pegasi. But first we need to collect our weapons and eat some breakfast. I'm sure you guys are starving." Their stomachs grumbled in reply.

They collected their things, and within the next few hours Diana cooked them a rabbit over a fire she made with her light powers, boiled them water from a nearby stream to drink, and crafted them makeshift belts for weapons out of the cloth bag they'd found them in. Everyone was given a dagger. Zoey kept the axe, and Andy took the sword. Spencer gathered as many berries as he could find for a snack later that day, while the pegasi grazed, and soon they were ready to visit the Fates.

Diana led Zoey to the smaller pegasus. "We'll ride Penelope," she said. Zoey smiled in awe at Penelope's shimmering white coat and stroked her silky mane. She'd never touched a horse before, although she'd always thought they were beautiful, but a pegasus was even more fascinating. Diana climbed onto Penelope's back, and Zoey followed suit.

Spencer jumped onto the back of the other pegasus and patted its neck. "C'mon, Andy. You can ride with me." Andy took slow, cautious steps toward them. Spencer chuckled. "No need to be afraid. Maia is a sweetheart."

Andy hoisted himself onto Maia's back. "How are we supposed to *not* fall off these things?"

Diana laughed. "Just hold on tight to Spencer and you should be fine." Andy gulped.

Zoey wrapped her arms around Diana's waist. "How long will it take to reach the Fates?"

"From here, and on pegasi, probably most of the day,"

Diana said. "Are you two ready?"

Zoey nodded. Her palms were sweaty, her heart palpitating. She'd never even ridden in a plane before, let alone on the back of a flying horse, but how else were they supposed to get more answers? She was scared, but she'd suck it up. It couldn't be worse than the end of the world.

Diana kicked Penelope's sides. "Go, Penny." The pegasus whinnied and flapped her wings. Zoey closed her eyes, her heart leaping in her chest as Penelope jumped off the ground. Soon crisp air bit her cheeks, her hair blowing behind her.

Zoey opened her eyes to see Andy clutching tight to Spencer as they flew alongside her and Diana through the clear blue sky. Below them, miles of endless forest swayed in the breeze. Behind, the ruins of her city grew smaller and smaller.

She shot Andy a glance. Although his eyes were full of fear, he offered her a small smile. Her stomach did flips as Penelope veered up and down, but she smiled back.

Until late afternoon they flew over the forest, only stopping once to let the pegasi graze while they snacked on berries. Eventually they reached a cliff where, at the bottom, a shallow stream ran into the jagged entrance of a cave.

Diana pointed at the cave. "There. That's where the Fates live." The pegasi descended toward the forest floor.

Once they landed next to the cave, they climbed to the ground. Diana lit her hands with a sphere of light. "Let's go," she said, and together they stepped into the darkness.

Immediately Zoey's shoes were soaked from the stream running through the cave. Every splash their steps made echoed off the walls, the only sight ahead a pitch-black abyss.

"Hello?" Diana called into the darkness, tossing the sphere of light between her hands. "Clotho? Lachesis? Atropos?"

Spencer walked beside Zoey, pulling the pegasi along by their reins. "Don't tell me they left this place after you and Syrena talked to them."

Diana turned and raised an eyebrow at Spencer. "And why do you think they would do that?"

Andy chewed the tip of his thumb. "Maybe they don't want us to save the world. Maybe they're against this whole thing."

The shrill, disembodied laugh of an old woman echoed off the walls. "What a foolish thing to say."

"Mortals are so entertaining," another cackled.

Diana perked up. "I knew they were still here. But . . ." She peered ahead. Even if someone was there, it was impossible to see. "May we see you? We want to talk to you. The mortals from the Before Time are here, just like the prophecy stated. You said you'd tell them what we needed to do."

"Of course, my dear, of course. We were looking forward to your return."

High-pitched cackles rang in Zoey's ears. The cave exploded with blue flashes, like fireworks in the sky, and the pegasi neighed in panic. Andy grabbed Zoey's arm. The ground began to tremble, then crumbled beneath their feet.

CHAPTER FIVE

THREAD

The air was thick with dust, and Andy's back ached from the impact of the fall, the wind knocked out of him. He caught his breath and groaned, then mustered the strength to sit up and shove the rocks off his body.

A quick look at his surroundings told him he wasn't in a cave anymore. It looked as though he was outside. His fingers brushed soft, dewy grass, and there were tall walls of vines and white petaled flowers. But there was no sky, only darkness above. *That must be where we fell through the cave floor*, he thought. In the center of the room or cavern or whatever the hell the place was, dim candles were scattered around a wooden spinning wheel.

His eyes watered. Dust had covered his glasses. He pulled them off and wiped them with his filthy sweatshirt as best he could, then put them back on and blinked a few more times, trying to adjust his vision. Upon closer inspection of the place, what appeared to be thousands—no, millions—of blue strings wove through the vine-and-flower walls and over the grass. They turned and twisted and knotted so much, Andy got a headache just thinking about trying to untangle them.

Beside him, Zoey coughed, rubbing her eyes. "Okay, what just happened?" On his other side, Spencer and Diana climbed to their feet and brushed the debris from their clothes, while above them, the pegasi whinnied and glided toward the room's grassy floor.

Familiar cackles rang through the air, tendrils of smoke curling up from the grass. The smoke grew taller and wider until finally it formed three bony old women in long robes. Their pupil-less eyes glowed blue, deep wrinkles spun into their skin like spiderwebs.

If three old women with glowing blue eyes had appeared from smoke on any normal day in Andy's life, he would have not only questioned his sanity, but also pissed his pants. However, this was not a normal day, and after all he'd seen thus far, they seemed totally average in comparison.

"Welcome," one said. She turned to Andy and Zoey. "We are the Fates. We've been waiting for your arrival. We see all; our power to see the destinies of mortals and gods alike surpass even Zeus himself. My name is Lachesis." Lachesis gestured at the second Fate, and she smiled, her teeth brown and crooked. "That is Clotho." She pointed toward the third Fate. "And that is Atropos." Atropos pulled a pair of scissors from her robes, knelt, and cut a few of the blue strings.

Andy and Zoey climbed to their feet. "I'm Andy, and this is Zoey," Andy said. "But I guess you probably already knew that." Lachesis chuckled.

Zoey gripped the axe at her belt. "If you see all, I have some questions for you. How did we get here from the past? How are we alive? And what's our fate?"

Lachesis stepped forward and pulled two glowing white strings from her robe pocket. They were tangled, knotted together to the point that they almost seemed like one string and not two. "There are many different outcomes to both of your fates, so whatever happens to you will be the result of your own choices. For now, all I can tell you is these are the threads that represent your lives. They are not like regular mortal threads. They are special."

Atropos gestured at the strings all around the room. "When we spin a new thread, mortal life is born. We watch over them, protect them, guide them, until it is time for them to die, in which case we cut their thread and they pass on to the next life. When you two died in the Storm, we went to cut your threads, but before we could, they turned white and began to glow. In that moment, we were given a vision of your potential future, and we knew we could not cut your threads just yet."

"Because we didn't cut them, your souls did not pass on to the next life," Lachesis said, stuffing the white strings back into her pocket. "Rather, they became dormant here on Earth."

"A few years after the gods took over, Apollo was given visions of your arrival, and the prophecy was born," Clotho said. "The gods were terrified of being overthrown, even if it seemed unlikely they would be by two mere mortals, but Zeus knew he had to take every precaution to keep his throne. Because the prophecy could only come true with the help of a demigod, he proposed all demigods be brought to and kept on Olympus by the age of ten. Convinced it was the only way to keep the prophecy from fruition, the gods agreed to his plan.

"The demigods were trained day in and day out, and forced to stay loyal to the gods and only the gods, or else they'd be deemed traitors and killed. All the while, your souls remained asleep until a demigod willing to sacrifice his or herself stepped up to bring you back. Syrena, the Daughter of Poseidon, fulfilled that part of the prophecy in an act of incredible selflessness for the world and all those she loved." At the mention of Syrena, Spencer glared at his feet, and Diana wiped tears from her eyes.

Zoey shifted her weight. "Why are our threads of life so special? You said they turned white and started to glow, but what does that mean?"

Lachesis stepped toward Zoey and pointed a long, crooked finger at her chest. "We cannot say. In time, you will discover it for yourself."

Zoey rolled her eyes. "All right. Fine. I guess that makes about as much sense as everything else in this whacked-out place. Now about the actual prophecy. It says we're going to lead a war on the gods. But we're just regular people.

We're not demigods, and we don't have special powers. How can we even hope to face off with them?"

Clotho laughed, making her way to the spinning wheel. "It does seem quite bleak, doesn't it?" She began fiddling with the wheel. "There are three gods, three brothers, who rule over the world. They are the most powerful in the entire Greek pantheon, and are feared by all. Those three are Hades, Poseidon, and Zeus. They each have an object of power, crafted for them specifically by the cyclopes during the war between the Titans and the gods. Their objects give them domain over the world. If you are to become worthy opponents of them, you must steal their objects of power. It's the only way you'll have a chance to defeat them. A slim chance, but a chance nonetheless."

Diana crossed her arms. "Let me guess. The first thing we need to do is travel to Hades, and they need to steal his object of power. The Helm of Darkness."

"Correct, Daughter of Apollo."

"We have to go to Hades? You mean like the underworld, where souls go when they die?" Andy asked, raising an eyebrow. "And we have to steal the Helm of Darkness? What's that?"

Clotho chuckled. "Yes, you must travel to where 'souls go when they die.' Spencer will know the way. It's in a place you once knew as the state of Utah."

"Utah? Why *Utah* of all places?" Andy said.

Spencer shrugged. "My father liked the scenery."

Clotho puckered her wrinkled lips and blew out a

cloud of smoke. It pulsed with blood-red light, and an ancient-looking charcoal helmet adorned with swirling designs shimmered inside it like a mystical mirage. "The Helm of Darkness is a helmet that clothes the wearer with complete invisibility, even to the gods, and whoever wears it can see any soul that resides in the underworld."

Andy's heart leapt in his chest. If he had the Helm, could he see his family again?

"Whoever wields the Helm controls Hades and what happens to the souls there," Clotho continued. She cleared her throat, and the cloud turned into a deep sea-blue, the Helm morphing into a three-pronged trident with jewels and pearls encrusted on the handle. "If you don't get killed stealing the Helm, the second thing you must do is travel to Poseidon's undersea palace. His object of power is the Trident. It can be used to cause earthquakes, and whoever wields it controls the oceans and the seas."

Again, she cleared her throat, and lightning flashed inside the cloud. Thunder followed. The cloud changed to peridot green, and the trident shifted into a solid, hissing gold lightning bolt. "The last object is the Lightning Bolt. It's located on New Mount Olympus, and it is the most powerful object in existence, surpassing the Helm and the Trident combined. With it you can create thunderstorms, and whoever wields it rules the world."

"Which is why they need to steal it last," Diana said. "They aren't even ready to face off with Hades yet, let alone Zeus himself."

Zoey raised an eyebrow. "Okay, I see where this plan could work in theory, but why does it have to be Andy and me that steal the objects? Why couldn't demigods just do it? Why did the prophecy have to go to all this trouble to bring us to life? It seems awfully counterproductive."

"In the old days, demigods could steal the objects," Atropos said, cutting a few more threads. "But after hearing the prophecy, Zeus couldn't take any chances with them. To avoid the demigods' rebellion, the gods worked together, using their powers to cast a spell on everything they possess that holds power so that demigods could not steal anything. If they even so much as touch one of the objects without permission, their life force will be sucked away, and they'll die. The wonderful thing about it all, though, is that the gods couldn't put the curse on regular mortals. They had to have a blood connection to cast the spell. So although the Son of Hades and the Daughter of Apollo cannot steal the objects, you, Zoey and Andrew, can."

"Not that they see you as much of a threat," Diana said. "They're more worried about demigods."

"But that still doesn't explain why we had to be brought back to life from the past," Zoey said. "Why couldn't the prophecy have picked some mortals from this time?"

Andy nodded, his eyes burning with tears as he thought of the people he'd lost. "Why us? Why me?"

"Again, I cannot say," Lachesis said. "In time, you will discover it for yourselves."

Atropos stopped cutting strings and cackled. "Oh, this

will be fun to watch. We saw you both in your old lives. It will be even more fun to watch you flounder in this one." Anger boiled in Andy's gut.

Clotho scowled. "Shut your blabbering mouth, Atropos. Why would you say something like that?"

Andy balled his fists. "I lost everything I knew, everyone I love, and you think it's *entertaining*?" He began to shake. "What if I decide I don't wanna go on this quest? What then? You could just cut my stupid thread already, right?"

Zoey grabbed his arm. "Andy, stop. You don't mean that."

He yanked his arm from her grasp. "They think our pain is funny. Is that not messed up to you at all?"

Atropos laughed and climbed to her feet, then faced Andy. "Now, now, child. There might be something in it for you."

Andy rolled his eyes. "Oh yeah? And what's that? Knowing deep in my heart I gave up everything to save the world? Yeah, not interested. Not if my family isn't even part of the world I'm saving."

"We have seen that if you, Andrew, go to Hades," she continued, "you may be presented with the opportunity to bring your family back to life."

Andy's jaw dropped, and everyone went silent. "If I go, they'll live?" he said. "My mom and my sister?"

"Whether it happens or not will be determined by the choices you make," Atropos said. "But Mark may also come back. And . . ." She smiled with her rotten brown teeth. "Your father will too."

Andy's heart stopped. "But my dad didn't die in the Storm. He died four years ag— I mean, before. From brain cancer."

"It does not matter," Atropos said. "We have seen the future. If you make the right decisions, you will be presented with the opportunity to save them all."

Andy let out a deep breath, goose bumps rising on his arms. "What about Zoey? What about her family? Her mother?"

Atropos shook her head. "This opportunity will only be for you, Andrew."

Andy bit his lip and hung his head. How was it fair that he was maybe going to get the chance to bring everyone he loved back, but Zoey wasn't? A soft hand took his, and he swung around to see Zoey as she gave him a warm smile. "It's okay. I've already accepted things as they are," she said. "I just hope this means you'll stop trying to get yourself killed."

Andy's eyes filled with tears. "I think it does. If there's a way to bring them back . . ." He choked on a cry. He'd do anything, *anything*, to bring them back. If he just had them again, he'd have a reason to fight. He'd have a reason to steal the objects of power. He'd have a reason to defeat the gods. He'd have a reason to live.

Zoey pulled away from him and turned to the Fates. "So how are we supposed to get into the underworld? And then get out? I mean, I'm guessing it isn't the easiest place to escape."

Lachesis gestured toward Spencer. "The Son of Hades grew up there. He knows who will be willing to help you." Spencer gave a slow nod.

Zoey frowned. "And how are we supposed to steal the Helm? I mean, we don't have any powers. We're just regular people."

Diana rested a hand on Zoey's shoulder. "You have our help. We'll guide you along the way and teach you how to fight."

Clotho rubbed her hands together. "Then it's settled. Your quest begins now. You will summon the one to help you in and out of Hades, travel there on your pegasi, and steal the Helm of Darkness."

"Thank you for all your help," Spencer said, then swung a fist into his palm. "Let's go."

The group turned to climb onto their pegasi to fly out of the Fates' lair, but Lachesis waved her hands in protest. "Wait, wait," she said. They swung around. "Before you go, we must create a veil around you to conceal you and your allies from the gods. Otherwise they will discover and destroy you before you even have a chance to fight them."

The group approached the Fates, and the three old women circled them and whispered an incoherent chant. Tendrils of smoke snaked toward the group, curling up and around their bodies, and Andy gasped, shocks of electricity whizzing across his skin. Once the Fates stopped, the smoke and shocks faded away.

Diana examined her arms. "How does this work? Did it make us completely invisible or something?"

"Not quite," Lachesis said. "If the gods find you in person, they will be able to see you. But they will not be able to summon themselves before you, nor will they be able to see you in their visions, unless you make a sacrifice to them or pray to them for help. Know this: once you pray to a god, even the veil will not be enough to hide you from said god. Choose your allies wisely."

"Good to know," Diana said. She bowed. "Thank you." The rest of the group bowed in thanks, then climbed onto the backs of Maia and Penelope and started their ascent.

The Fates waved to them. "Good luck," they said in unison, and disappeared in a cloud of smoke.

After the group made it back into the cave, they hopped off their pegasi and walked back to the entrance. By the time they reached the outside, the sky was bright with a colorful sunset.

Andy squinted. "So who are we supposed to talk to now? Someone to help us in and out of Hades?"

Spencer nodded. "Tomorrow we'll gather some berries and build a small fire as a sacrifice to summon her. But for now, we should make camp, eat, and sleep. You two have been through a lot in one day."

"Summon her?" Zoey said. "Don't tell me she's a goddess."

"She's a goddess," Spencer said, crossing his arms.

"But don't worry. It's my stepmother. She's like a mom to me, since I never knew my real mother. She's not like most of the other gods."

Diana snapped her fingers. "Oh, that's perfect." She turned to Zoey and Andy. "Her name is Persephone, Goddess of Spring. Hades kidnapped her in the old days and forced her to be his wife, and she became Queen of the Underworld. Her mom, Demeter, Goddess of Harvest, got upset and didn't let anything grow until Zeus agreed to free her. But because she ate some pomegranate seeds from the underworld, she was bound to it."

"Exactly why I know she'll help us," Spencer said. "For six months out of the year, she's allowed to be with Demeter. But for the other six months, she has to be in the underworld. She hates it. I remember that when I lived there, one of her only joys of staying was to see me."

Andy nibbled on his thumb. "I think I may have heard that myth before in an article on the internet or something. It's the ancient Greek explanation for the seasons, right? When Persephone was free, Demeter was happy, so everything was growing and beautiful. Spring and summer. When she was trapped in the underworld, her mom was sad, so everything died. Fall and winter."

Diana shot Andy a glare. "Call it a myth again and I'll blast you to the other side of the forest."

Andy laughed and raised his hands in surrender. "Jeez, okay, sorry."

By sunset's end, the group found a place to camp and

ate dinner. Spencer stayed awake to watch for monsters while the rest of them slept.

The next morning, they walked through lush forest, gathering berries, twigs, and grass for their sacrifice to Persephone. Soon they'd gathered more than enough, stuffing it all in Diana's pack, then began the search for the perfect place to summon her.

"As a Goddess of Spring, she'll have more power to manifest herself and will be able to talk to us longer if we summon her in a place where her symbols of power are present," Spencer said. "She's especially powerful around waterfalls, certain flowers, willow trees, and pomegranates."

"I think right now our best bet is a waterfall," Diana said. "When I was out here with Syrena, I saw quite a few."

They approached a wide clearing in the forest, tons of pine trees cut down in a lopsided circle. Five little huts made of branches, pine needles, and mud were clustered together in the opening. Rags Andy assumed were clothing hung from ropes strung between them, and wind whistled through the surrounding trees.

Andy raised an eyebrow. "Huh. That's totally not creepy at all."

Diana halted, motioning for them to do the same, then drew her bow. Spencer clutched his spear. Zoey grasped her axe. Andy cocked his head, listening for whatever they'd detected. A twig cracked, and the first person he'd seen since meeting Diana and Spencer darted out from one of the huts.

It was a young girl dressed in rags, with long, stringy blonde hair. She looked as frail as a brittle leaf, her cloudy blue eyes sunken into her skull, her gray skin hanging limply from her bones. Andy guessed she was around Mel-Mel's age—eight years old—and a pang of grief shot through his chest at the memory of her. *But if the Fates are right, I won't have to be sad anymore*, he thought. *I might get my sister back.*

The young girl fell at Diana's feet. "Please, please— don't hurt me," she said in a small, weak voice. "They killed my family, my parents . . ."

"Who killed your family?" Diana said.

The girl shook her head, tears rolling down her cheeks. She'd lost everyone she loved, just like Andy, except she wasn't going to get even the slimmest chance to see them again. With that realization, he felt the need to comfort her.

He stepped forward and knelt beside her. "Hey, it's okay. You're safe now. What's your name?"

"Vanessa," she whimpered. "Who are you?"

"I'm Andy," he said, then gestured toward everyone else. "That's Zoey, Diana, Spencer, Maia, and Penelope." The pegasi nickered at the mention of their names. Andy took Vanessa's hands in his own. They were like the cold, breakable hands of a porcelain doll. "I need you to do something for me, Vanessa. I need you to tell us who killed your family."

She gulped. "They were birds. Big, big birds."

Spencer rubbed his temple. "Great."

"What is it?" Zoey said.

Diana glared at the sky. "If it was the Stymphalian Birds, we need to get out of here, and fast." But Andy didn't want to leave. He wanted to protect Vanessa.

He cupped her cheeks in his palms. "I know you're scared. But I'll make sure no more children lose their parents like you did. I'll get rid of those birds, and you'll be safe." She nodded, a smile tugging at the corners of her mouth. It filled Andy with a familiar warmth he hadn't felt since the world ended.

"Andy," Spencer said, "I need to speak with you for a moment." Confused, Andy turned and stood, then made his way to Spencer's side.

Spencer took him by the shoulders and pulled him away from Vanessa. "I don't think you understand the ramifications of telling a little girl you're going to kill what could be the Stymphalian Birds for her when we haven't even trained you yet."

Andy pulled himself from Spencer's grasp. "I get that we haven't trained, but Zoey and I killed that Harpy without even knowing what was going on. Plus, aren't we supposed to save the world? From gods?"

Zoey eyed the trees and put a hand on her hip. "I think Spencer might be right, Andy. We haven't been trained. We have no idea what we're up against. Not to say we can't take her with us and keep her safe, I just don't think we should be hunting monsters yet."

Diana turned to Andy, her bow and arrow ready still. "Did you not hear Vanessa say they killed her family? They aren't like the Harpy—I had been fighting her off for days, and she was all alone. They're in a flock, they're huge, their feathers are crazy sharp and can be used to attack their enemies, they eat people, and their droppings are acidic. Back in the old days, one of the greatest heroes in all of Greece, Heracles, had to kill them because no one else could. And believe me, we're nothing compared to him. So forgive me if I'm wrong, but you two need to be kept as safe as possible, especially until you've had some proper training. Which means no looking for trouble."

"How did Heracles defeat the birds?" Andy asked.

"He scared them out of their nests and shot them with poison-laced arrows," Spencer said. "But we don't have any poisonous arrows. And we don't know where they're nesting."

Vanessa's scream of terror pierced the air, while the pegasi flapped their wings and whinnied. Andy looked to the sky. A flock of giant ebony swans flew toward the clearing, visible just beyond the tall trees. Their shiny feathers shifted between black and silver in the sunlight. Their beaks were a dull bronze, their red eyes gleaming with malice. Together they let out a screech, and the trees shook.

Spencer's jaw dropped. "That's them. The Stymphalian Birds."

A bird the size of a school bus swooped down. It landed on the forest floor and crushed a hut under its talons. Vanessa screamed. In one quick movement the monster snatched her with its beak.

Andy didn't have time to feel the panic rushing through his body, or the racing of his frantic heart. He had to save Vanessa, and he had to do it *now*, training or no training. He unsheathed his sword and charged for the monster. Before he could reach it, it slammed its wings down, and a gust of powerful wind sent him flying backward. He cried, "Vanessa!" and crashed into the grass. The rest of the group rushed to his side. The bird took flight, spiraling into the sky to join its friends. Andy climbed to his feet and watched in utter shock.

Vanessa was gone.

"C'mon, we have to get out of here," Diana said.

The group bolted toward Maia and Penelope, but the pegasi had already flown into the sky. Four of the birds broke away from the flock and blocked the pegasi's path, then seized them by their bellies with bronze beaks. Red blood splattered all over their white coats, and they wrestled against the birds, neighing and screaming until their eyes dulled and their bodies went limp.

"Penny! Maia!" Zoey said. Her eyes filled with tears, and Andy's stomach fell to his feet. What were they supposed to do now?

"Run!" Diana yelled, and they swung around and dashed pell-mell for the trees. Three more birds swooped down in front of them. They crushed the rest of the huts under their talons, and when they flapped their wings, more wind sent the group tumbling back. They crashed into the forest floor in a violent swirl of grass and dirt. The birds screeched in unison, shaking the forest, and they scrambled to their feet. They turned to run in the other direction, but two more birds blocked the way.

Diana and Spencer readied their weapons. "Zoey, Andy," Spencer said, "whatever you do, do *not* get yourselves killed." The demigods hurtled toward the monsters. Spencer stabbed one in a beady red eye, while Diana sent arrows at another's head. Zoey waved her axe. One of the smaller birds stomped toward her, and she hacked its throat.

A few tears trickled down Andy's cheeks, his head spinning. When he'd found out everyone he loved was dead, he'd been so distraught he'd wanted to stay dead with them. But now he had the chance to see them again. If he could just get to Hades, maybe he could save them.

That alone was enough to make him want to fight for his life, but on top of that, the birds had eaten Maia, Penelope, and Vanessa. Vanessa, a scared, helpless little girl, a victim of the gods' cruelty. He'd been determined to protect her, but he'd failed.

A new sensation overcame him. A burning anger brewed in his gut. Every vein in his body coursed with boiling energy, and the need to tear the Stymphalian Birds to shreds made his fingers twitch.

He let out a cry, a cry from the pit of his terror and anger, then sprinted into battle. Everything but the birds faded into a blur around him. A scrawny one as tall as a small car screeched in his face, its saliva spraying his cheeks. He mustered all his strength and swung his sword. The blade sliced through its neck, and its head tumbled to the side, blood squirting from the stump.

To his right, Spencer said, "Heads up!" and he looked to the sky. A string of green droppings soared toward them. Zoey and Diana somersaulted to the side, and Andy ducked behind his shield. The droppings splattered against it. It seared and sizzled, the straps heating as if someone had lit the other side on fire. He shrieked and ripped it off his arm, then tossed it aside. The center melted into the forest floor like butter in a scalding pan.

He remembered Diana saying the birds had acidic droppings, and cursed himself for not jumping out of the way. Before he could finish his slew of cuss-words, an especially large and ugly bird with patches of feathers missing swung around and seized him with its bronze beak. He screamed, losing grip of his sword, and the weapon fell to the ground as he slid to the back of the bird's mouth. It took flight, slamming its beak shut, enveloping him in slimy darkness that reeked worse than a decomposing skunk.

His heart raced, his shaking hands searching for something to clasp, only slipping over gooey saliva. "Have you heard of breath mints?" he yelled, falling farther down the bird's skinny throat.

He racked his brain for an idea, anything to get him out of its body. His fingers brushed the cold, smooth knife handle on his belt. He snatched the dagger and sank it into the bird's neck, anchoring himself. It shrieked. The walls of its esophagus shook. He planted his feet against the other side and twisted his dagger to slice open a way of escape. A sliver of morning sunlight poked through its throat. With as much strength as he could muster, he tore through the last of its muscles and arteries and flesh.

He screamed, tumbling through the sky.

CHAPTER SIX

STEPMOTHER

Branches slapped Andy's body, slowing his fall. Pine needles scratched his skin. He hit the ground. His glasses flew off his face, and sharp pains racked his body, the air knocked from his lungs. He gasped for breath. He clawed the ground, grabbed his glasses, and put them back on.

"Andy!" Zoey screamed. He looked to the side to see Zoey running toward him, her long brown curls blowing behind her like the cape of a superhero.

Beside her, a bird chopped the air with its wings and sent a cluster of glittering feathers spiraling toward her head. She threw up her shield. The feathers pierced it. She stumbled to the side and collided with Diana. The bird shrieked and flapped after them, and Diana launched a sphere of light toward it. The sphere blasted the bird's head, and chunks of bones and brains splattered across the ground, the headless body collapsing in a bloody heap. A few of its friends screeched, then ruffled their feathers and swarmed Zoey and Diana.

Andy caught his breath and groaned, climbing to his knees. Where was his dagger? His sword? They needed his help.

A bird the size of a motorcycle leapt in front of him, shrieking in his face, and he scrambled backward. Pain shot through his bones. He cried out. The bird knocked him down and pressed him into the grass with its talons, clacking its beak at his throat. He clawed the ground with trembling hands and seized a jagged rock. He gritted his teeth and mustered the last of his strength, then pounded the rock into the bird's skull. It bit his shoulder, but he hit its head again. It screeched and drew back.

He climbed to his feet, his breaths shallow. His vision was blurred. His head throbbed, his bones ached, his shoulder stung. He didn't know how he was supposed to go on fighting. It was hard to stand. Hard to keep his eyes open.

The bird gathered its composure, its red eyes flashing with hunger. It let out a triumphant squawk and advanced on him.

This is it, he thought. *This is how I die.*

He thought of his mother, of his sister, of Mark. He imagined the fear and hopelessness they must have felt in their last moments, and then he thought of his father on the night he died of cancer. *I promise you'll all be just fine. So long as you have each other.*

If he couldn't fight now, there was no chance of saving them later. He'd never be fine. Not without the people he loved.

He couldn't let that happen.

He sucked in a deep breath, his body pulsing with new strength. Before the bird could reach him, he dashed around it and leapt onto its back. It screamed, craning its neck to bite him. He slammed the rock against its temple once, twice, three times. Its skull cracked. It choked for breath, something deep in its throat gurgling, and then it collapsed.

He scrambled away from the body and climbed to his feet, shocked and thankful he wasn't the one dead on the ground.

More of the flock shrieked from the sky. A chill shot down his back. He didn't have either of his weapons or his shield. A single rock wouldn't cut it if he had to fight many more of those things.

He looked toward the clearing to find Zoey, Diana, and Spencer standing close together. Scrapes and bruises covered Zoey's body. Blood and guts dripped from Spencer's weapon and hers. Diana had used the last of her arrows. Andy darted between dead bodies and made his way to their side, rock in hand.

Sweat rolled down Diana's face. She gasped for breath, her cheeks even paler than usual. "If you guys take cover, I can use my sunlight powers to kill the rest of them."

Spencer grabbed her shoulder, panic in his dark-brown eyes. "No, don't. If you use too much of your strength, you could kill yourself."

She plucked his hand off her shoulder. "I know." She tossed her bow aside and lifted her hands to the sky. A look of fear came over her freckled face. "I know I betrayed you, Dad. But please, help me. Please lend me the strength to defeat the Stymphalian Birds. If you don't, I could die."

Spencer ran for the trees, gesturing for Andy and Zoey to follow. "C'mon!"

"What's happening?" Andy said. "Is Diana going to be okay?" The birds swooped down. Zoey grabbed Andy's hand. They sprinted for the trees.

Behind them, Diana roared like a lion. Andy looked over his shoulder and caught a glimpse of tiny clouds of smoke floating from her parted lips.

Andy and Zoey leapt into the trees and dropped onto their stomachs next to Spencer. Diana stood in the clearing. They gazed in awe as her blonde hair became yellow fire, and flames danced from her eyes, mouth, and hands. The birds swarmed her. Their cries shook the forest floor. Their wings sent gusts of wind that blasted Andy's face. They screeched and clacked their beaks at Diana. Her body lit up with flames, and she exploded with golden light, sending the birds flying in all directions.

Andy ducked. A few of the birds grazed his hair and barreled through clusters of trees, sharp branches impaling their bodies. He squinted, trying to find Diana, but she wasn't there anymore. Instead, where she once stood, a line of fiery golden sunlight shot into the sky like a monstrous volcanic eruption. The light grew so bright and hot he had to close his eyes.

When the heat finally died, he opened them. Smoke billowed through the clearing. Where the birds had been blasted into the forest, trees were ripped from their roots, and the remainder of the flock flew away, leaving the casualties behind without a second glance.

In the center of the clearing, Diana stood, her chin lifted high, her arms raised. She was—quite literally—on fire. She let out a soft whimper and collapsed, and the flames of her body died.

Spencer and Zoey jumped to their feet and raced toward her. "Diana!" Spencer cried. Andy struggled to stand. He limped behind them, his body aching.

Spencer knelt next to Diana and brushed her cheek with the back of his hand. But she didn't wake up, and a sense of dread overcame Andy. Had she killed herself, like Spencer suggested she might?

For a few moments they sat in unnerving silence, before finally, Diana's green eyes fluttered open. "My dad really pulled through this time," she said, coughing between words. "I'm a traitor, and he still gave me the power to save the day." Spencer hugged her, and Andy sighed in relief.

Zoey threw her hands into the air. "What *was* that?"

Diana trembled, her breaths heavy. She pulled herself to her feet and brushed herself off. "You mean my powers?" Zoey nodded.

Spencer rested a hand on Diana's shoulder. "If you're

a demigod, whatever powers you may have come from your godly parent. The closer you are to what gives you power, the stronger your abilities are. The farther from what gives you power, the weaker your abilities are. Diana is a Daughter of Apollo. He's the god of a lot of things, including sunlight and healing. And those are the powers she inherited from him. She conjures sunlight, and she heals."

"Well, I figured out that much. But she was on fire," Zoey said, then faced Diana. "Why did you have to ask your dad to help you? Why did Spencer say you might kill yourself? That was terrifying."

Diana chuckled weakly and took a deep breath. "Demigods get tired when we use too much of our power, even if we're close to what gives us strength. We can burn up our bodies and kill ourselves. When I first discovered I had the ability to set myself ablaze and blast things into oblivion, I almost died. But my dad was watching over me. He saved me. So I asked him for help today, even though I didn't know if he'd be willing to give any, considering our relationship isn't all sunshine and rainbows lately." She winked. "We'd have been bird food if I didn't do *something*, and better me die than you or Andy."

Spencer cracked a smile. "Just don't do that again. You had me pretty worried."

Diana elbowed his side. "Don't tell me what to do."

Andy furrowed his brow. "What do we do now that the birds got Maia and Penelope?"

"Damn it all to Tartarus," Diana said, shooting the sky a glare. "We'll have to walk everywhere now."

"We need to get our things together and summon my stepmother," Spencer said. "Maybe she can help us figure something out."

Diana took a few more minutes to recover, but once she was back to normal, she healed Andy's and Zoey's injuries. She gave Andy her shield, insisting he needed it more than she did and scolding him for letting the first one get destroyed. They gathered their weapons, then continued the walk to a place where they could summon Persephone and come up with a solid plan to enter and exit the underworld without the help of their lost pegasi.

They trudged on late into the day, gathering more berries, twigs, and grass, since during the fight with the Stymphalian Birds most of it had fallen out of Diana's pack and was destroyed. Soon they reached a small waterfall flowing into a stream at the bottom of a cliff.

"This is the perfect place to reach her," Spencer said, and they crawled to the bottom.

Spencer made a pile of twigs and grass and looked to Diana. "Can you start a fire for me?" She nodded and blasted it with a small sphere of light, and it went up in crackling flames. Spencer dropped a handful of berries into the fire. "Persephone, it's your one and only stepson, Spencer. Please accept my sacrifice and make yourself present to me. I need your guidance."

At first nothing happened, the only sound the stream

whispering as it ran farther into the forest. Andy swallowed hard, anxious as to what they were supposed to do if Persephone didn't show up. Would they still be able to go to Hades, or would they abandon the quest altogether? Knowing that traveling to the underworld was the only way he may ever see his family again, he prayed to whatever deity that wasn't a total psychopath he'd be able to get there.

The fire sighed, and its flames retreated. From the curling smoke a girl who couldn't be older than sixteen took form, wildflowers sprouting from the grass at her feet.

She was petite, only a few inches taller than Diana, with a soft, curvy figure accentuated by a shimmering yellow dress that reached the ground. Her chestnut-brown hair was piled on her head in a bun made of braids and curls, a few wispy pieces framing her hazel eyes and pink cheeks.

When she saw Spencer, she gave him a dazzling white smile and ran into his outstretched arms. "Spencer!" she cried, her voice as youthful as her appearance.

Andy couldn't believe the Queen of the Underworld was just a teenage girl. He thought she'd be tall and cold and calculating. He thought she'd be someone who looked as if they'd smite a person down without hesitation. But Persephone looked sweet and warm. He could imagine her as a girl in his high school, spending her free time with a few close friends in libraries and coffee shops.

Spencer pulled out of their hug, his eyes serious. "It's so good to see you again, stepmother. I only wish it were under better circumstances."

Persephone narrowed her eyes at Diana. "Why are you with the Daughter of Apollo? Zeus wants her captured. What's the meaning of this?"

Spencer dropped to his knees and took her hands. "Please, before you get angry, hear me out," he said. She looked down at him with worried eyes. "You hate the months you have to spend in Hades each year, don't you?"

She raised her eyebrows, as if confused. "Well, of course. But you already know that. Why?"

"What if I told you you'd never have to go back?"

Her pouty lips drew into a small smile. "I'm listening."

Spencer stood, squeezing her hands. "Syrena allowed herself to be executed as an act of sacrifice. That sacrifice resurrected two mortals from the Before Time, the two mortals of the prophecy."

Persephone gasped, her eyes widening. "*The* prophecy?"

Spencer nodded. "*The* prophecy. Obviously, as you know, mortals aren't exactly—*equipped* to fight gods. Or even demigods, really. But the Fates gave us a plan that would grant them the power to become worthy opponents of the gods. They have to steal the Helm of Darkness, the Trident, and the Lightning Bolt. Only then can they fight the gods, and we plan to help them do it."

Persephone's jaw fell. She pulled away from Spencer and hugged her sides. "You plan to overthrow the Olympians." Her voice cracked as she said it. "But why?"

Spencer threw his hands in the air. "Think about all

they've done to us. Think about the fact that you have to stay married to my father for the rest of eternity."

"It is quite dreadful," Persephone said. "I've never loved him, you know."

Diana stepped toward the goddess. "If you help us get in and out of Hades, we'll make sure you never have to go back to the underworld. You could roam the earth as you please. You could fall in love with someone wonderful." Persephone bit her lip and watched the waterfall for a few minutes. Andy held his breath, sharing a look of concern with Zoey.

Persephone turned back to Spencer and Diana. "You'll need a lot of silver drachmas to ride the ferry across the Acheron, and you'll need something to transport you out of the underworld once you've stolen the Helm. Do you have any idea how you're going to steal it without getting killed?"

"We had a few ideas," Diana said. "But Spencer hoped you could help us with that."

Persephone frowned. "Perhaps, if I paid my husband a visit and provided a distraction of some sort, you could sneak into the castle and steal it when he's not paying attention."

Diana snapped her fingers. "That's perfect."

Persephone brushed the wispy curls behind her ears. "Yes, yes. I think it could work, provided the timing is right." She bit her lip. "We must hurry. How are you going to travel there? Do you have any pegasi?"

Spencer hung his head. "No. We had two from Olympus, but we were attacked by the Stymphalian Birds. They were killed."

"Syrena and I stole some, too. We rode them all the way out here," Diana added. "But one of the Harpies that came after us managed to set them free after the other kidnapped Syrena. They could be anywhere now, even eaten by monsters."

Persephone rested a hand on Spencer's shoulder. "Not to worry. There's a village I've passed over a few times on my way to Hades, and they have pegasi. Deltama Village. You could reach it on foot within the next five or six days. Perhaps they'll be willing to lend you a few if you explain why you need them. If you must, I'm sure you could steal some. From there it would take only a day to reach the underworld."

"How do we get to Deltama Village?" Spencer asked.

"Follow the setting sun until you see the tall log gates," Persephone said, her form twitching like a glitch in a computer screen. "I must go. My power is dwindling." She wiggled her fingers, and with a flash of yellow light, two black sacks manifested in her palms. One was fat and jingled like a sack of quarters, while the other looked small and shriveled. She handed them to Spencer and kissed his cheek. "Use the drachmas to get across the Acheron. Eat the pomegranate seeds to escape the underworld once you've completed your mission. After the night is over, you have nine days, my child."

Her form twitched again, and she disintegrated, leaving behind only the smell of smoke.

CHAPTER SEVEN

VISIONS

After Persephone disappeared, Diana declared Zoey and Andy would begin their training.

They speed-walked through the trees, looking for a clearing of sorts, and Zoey's heart hammered with anticipation. Fighting the Stymphalian Birds without knowing what to do had been terrifying, and she'd received her fair share of injuries. If it weren't for Diana and Spencer's efforts to protect them, she was sure they would have died in the attack. But she hoped learning how to fight would, with time, help them become a force to be reckoned with.

Just as the sun began to set, they found a wide field of hills and wildflowers.

"This will do," Spencer said.

Zoey pulled her axe from her belt and took the leather cover off. "What are we going to learn first?" She swung it through the air, a satisfying *swoosh* bringing a grin to her lips. "Are you gonna show us any special techniques, or should we just start sparring?"

Spencer shared a knowing look with Diana, then patted Zoey on the shoulder. Her cheeks grew hot. "Slow down," he said, and pulled away from her. "Just take a seat."

Andy plopped onto his butt and sighed. "Oh, thank God."

Zoey hesitated, then returned her axe to the belt and sat next to Andy. "I thought we were going to start our training."

Diana put her hands on her hips. "You are."

Spencer crossed his arms. "We don't have a lot of time to train you guys using conventional methods. There's no way you'll be ready to go into the underworld in only nine days, not to mention there's still a chance you'll have to fight one of the three most powerful gods to ever exist, even if you steal his object of power."

"I was finally feeling hopeful," Andy said. "Way to burst my bubble."

"Which is why," Spencer continued, "we're going to train you in the most efficient way possible." He paused, his expression growing dark. "I'm going to give you visions of the times I've been in combat."

Zoey tugged on her tangled curls. "Okay. But how do we learn anything from that? We'll just be watching you fight. We won't be doing anything."

"That's not true," Spencer said. "When I conjure visions of events that I wasn't involved in, the person seeing the vision watches it play out as an outsider. But when I conjure visions of events that I was part of, the person seeing the vision experiences everything I knew and felt in those moments, and the knowledge you receive will remain."

Andy adjusted his glasses and smiled. "Badass, badass."

Zoey furrowed her brow. "So we're basically going to be completely immersed as you in your memories." Spencer nodded. "Will we automatically know what we're doing in a fight because of it? Like, will we adopt your habits and skills?"

"Only during the vision," Spencer said. "Once you're out, you'll still have access to the knowledge, but you'll have to tap into it yourself. We'll spar after every vision I give you, and we'll see how you improve over these nine days."

Zoey squared her shoulders. "I'm ready."

"Me too," Andy said.

Spencer sat before them and pressed his thumbs against their foreheads. "Here we go." In an instant, an ocean of fog consumed Zoey.

As quickly as it came, it cleared, and she somersaulted through a black abyss. The sound of heavy rain echoed in the darkness. She felt as though her body were being compressed into a tiny vent, and upward she flew.

Suddenly she was sprinting in the middle of a forest not too different from the one she'd been in all day. The sky was gray. Rain poured down, soaking her from head to toe, and she shivered from the cold. Thunder rumbled.

Running beside her was a beautiful girl much shorter

than her. She had deep-olive skin, long brown curls, and sharp hazel eyes. The girl was Syrena, Daughter of Poseidon. And she had more love in her heart for the girl than she'd ever had for anyone else. They'd been dating for years. She'd do anything for the girl, anything. Including die for her.

A young man was on Zoey's other side. He was shorter than her too, with gold eyes and a lightning scar on his face and neck. Karter, Son of Zeus. They'd been best friends ever since she'd been brought to Olympus. He'd been happier back then, more carefree, and he hadn't looked so scary. He was the brother she'd never had. She'd do anything for him, too.

They'd been in the rain for hours, looking for a group of seven men and women who'd escaped Ares City with the intention of starting their own settlement far into the country. It had angered and embarrassed Ares, the God of War, and Zeus had decided it was time he sent his best team of demigod warriors to slaughter the men and women, every last one of them, for their betrayal of the gods.

A man's battle cry sounded from above. Zoey looked up just in time to see five of the men and women sitting high in the trees. The traitors readied their bows and shot an army of arrows straight for them.

She ducked and raised her shield, blocking the attack. Syrena drew a whip of water from a pouch at her side and slapped the arrows away, while Karter flew into the air and darted between the projectiles as they whizzed down.

More battle cries came from behind. She looked over her shoulder to see two men running toward her, weapons in hand. She screamed in fury and sprinted for them. How dare they betray the gods!

The first thrust his sword at her, but she blocked it with the shaft of her spear and plunged her weapon through his chest. The second sent a knife spiraling toward her head, and she threw up her shield. The blade bounced off it. She ripped her spear from the first man's bloody chest, and he fell on his face.

The second man lunged for her. She shoved the tip of her spear through his throat. He coughed and choked, blood spurting from his wound, before his eyes went blank. She pulled her weapon back to her side.

She paused. She'd been training to kill people since she'd arrived on Olympus, but she'd never actually taken a life until now. She thought she'd feel powerful, strong, proud. But something about the blood pooling around the men's dead bodies, something about the dullness in their eyes, made her stomach churn.

She shook her head, willing her feelings to go away. She had orders. Orders to make sure they were all dead. If she didn't follow through with those orders, *her* punishment would be death. Or worse.

Before she could race back to Syrena's and Karter's sides, before she could help them more, fog appeared in the corners of her vision and consumed her again.

The fog cleared, and Spencer pulled away from them,

beads of sweat running down his face. Zoey gasped for breath and dug her nails into the grass beneath her. Where was Syrena? Karter? She had to help them . . . She had to . . .

Wait, no. It was just a vision. Spencer's memory.

She closed her eyes. She'd already figured that Karter had been one of Spencer's best friends, based on the confrontation they'd had when they'd found her and Andy. But she'd had no idea Syrena had been his long time girlfriend. The dead girl everyone kept talking about, the one who'd sacrificed herself to bring Zoey and Andy back to life . . .

Why Spencer had betrayed Karter to help her and Andy succeed in their quest suddenly made so much more sense.

She shivered. She had to focus on the task at hand, not try to dissect Spencer's motives for helping them. A little girl had lost her life today. Penelope and Maia had lost their lives too. She had to learn how to fight so that no one else would die. So that she could steal the objects of power. So that she could become a worthy opponent of the gods.

She shared an uneasy look with Andy. "That was intense," Andy whispered.

Diana stood behind Spencer, her hands on her hips. "Did you learn anything?"

"I'm not sure," Andy said.

Zoey gulped. "I think I did."

Spencer climbed to his feet, and Diana gestured for

her to stand. "Then get up. It's time to spar."

Zoey followed Diana and Spencer to the middle of the field, her axe in her right hand, her shield strapped to her left. They fought, Diana throwing spheres of light at her, instructing her to block them with her shield, while at the same time Zoey clashed her axe against Spencer's spear. She tried to connect with the vision Spencer had given them, to unlock the knowledge he'd already possessed in battle, but in less than a minute they knocked her axe to the side and her on her butt, her hair plastered against her forehead with sweat.

Spencer offered her a hand. Her heart skipped a beat, and she took it. He helped her to her feet. "I guess I didn't learn as much as I thought," she said with a sigh.

Spencer shook his head. "That was pretty good, considering you're a beginner, and you're fighting against highly trained demigods with powers. We'll keep working on it."

She pulled her hand from his, fiddled with a strand of hair, and looked down at her shoes. They were disgustingly filthy, covered in dried blood and dirt. "Um— Uh— Thanks."

Diana gestured at Andy to join them. "All right, Andy, I don't care if you didn't learn anything. It's your turn." Andy stood and made his way toward the demigods, sword and shield in hand, while Zoey took his spot on the sidelines.

They sparred against Andy, much like they had with

Zoey. In less than a minute his sword was knocked aside and he was on the ground.

Spencer offered him a hand. "We'll keep working on it." Andy allowed Spencer to help him to his feet.

The sun had nearly finished setting. "It's been a long, perilous day of adventuring," Diana said. "Let's cut training short tonight, have dinner, and go to bed. When the sun rises in the morning, we'll start our walk to Deltama Village, and we'll train every day before dinner."

They all agreed to her proposal, and soon she was cooking them another rabbit over a smoking campfire in the trees. Spencer prepared roots and berries to eat. By the time the group finished their feast, clusters of radiant stars shone in the dark sky. A raven called in the distance.

Spencer fixed his gaze on the crackling fire. "You two defended yourselves well today against the Stymphalian Birds, considering you had no idea what you were doing. I'm impressed."

Zoey flashed him a smile, but Andy frowned and hung his head. "I just wish we could have saved Vanessa," he said.

Spencer slumped his shoulders. "Sometimes we can't save everyone. But we have to go on. We can't let them die in vain." Andy gave a slow nod.

Diana's eyes filled with tears. She bit her lip, then buried her face in her hands and fell into a fit of sobs.

"What's wrong?" Spencer asked.

Diana sniffled. "What you said—'we can't let them die

in vain'—well, I mean, it just made me think of Syrena."

Spencer narrowed his eyes in an icy glare. "Shut up."

"I haven't talked about her at all," Diana said, wiping her cheeks with her dress. "I'm practically acting like she didn't exist. I have to talk about her, at least a little bit. I have to grieve."

Spencer shook his head and stood. "Then I can't be here right now. I just . . ." His voice wavered. He spun around and stomped farther into the trees. Zoey exchanged a worried glance with Andy.

"Don't worry, he'll come back," Diana said. "He just needs some time. He probably can't believe she's dead. I know I can't."

Andy scooted next to Diana and patted her back. "I know we kind of just met, but if you want to talk about it, I'm here to listen."

Zoey glanced at the trees where Spencer had stomped off. *Why is he being such a jerk to Diana?* Her heart skipped, her stomach twisting with nausea. She'd felt exactly how he'd felt about Syrena that day during the vision. She already knew the answer.

She turned to Diana. "Me too."

Diana's lip quivered. "Syrena was one of my best friends. She was Spencer's girlfriend. She was amazing and selfless, always thinking about people who needed her help, always there for anyone who needed a friend. I loved her. I loved her so much, and she's gone." She stared into the fire, her expression blank, more tears trickling down her cheeks. "I just don't know what we're going to do without her."

Zoey and Andy nodded, and for a few minutes they didn't say anything. Zoey was about to break the silence and ask Diana more about the times she'd spent with Syrena, before Andy opened his mouth to speak. "Wait a second," he said, cocking his head. "If Spencer is the Son of Hades, and Syrena was the Daughter of Poseidon, wouldn't that make Spencer and Syrena cousins?" Diana wiped her tears and raised an eyebrow. "Wouldn't that make all of you related? Is it not weird that two cousins were dating?" Zoey grimaced. She hadn't thought about it that way.

Diana's confused gaze drifted between them before she exploded with laughter. "Oh my gods— Regular mortals are so— No, it's not weird at all. The gods aren't human. They aren't made of the same flesh humans are. They marry their own siblings all the time. But it's not like a human marrying their brother or sister. As long as demigods don't share the same god or human parent, it's not weird at all to date."

Zoey gave a nervous laugh. "That might take a while to get used to."

"No kidding," Andy said.

They talked for a long time about nothing in particular, and by the end of their conversation, Diana seemed to be feeling much better. Although her eyes were still sad, she was making an effort to smile and laugh. She stayed awake to watch for monsters, and Andy rested his head against a patch of grass and fell asleep.

Zoey told Diana she needed to go to the bathroom, which was a lie, and made her way through the trees in the direction Spencer had left. The truth was, she wanted to look for him. He'd been a jerk, but she was sick with worry for him for a reason she hadn't yet come to understand.

Pine needles pricked her arms. She chopped branches with her axe, the moon and stars barely lighting her surroundings as the dying campfire grew farther and farther away.

For a while she walked in silence, before finally a twig snapped ahead. "Spencer?" she called, scanning the forest for any sign of him.

"Zoey? Is that you?" a voice that must have belonged to him called back.

"Yeah, it's me. Where are you?"

"Keep walking."

Zoey pressed on, hacking branches with her axe. Soon she reached a cluster of boulders covered in dense moss, trees hanging over them. Spencer sat atop the tallest, his chiseled features illuminated under the moonlight. He offered her a smile, though his eyes were sad, and gestured for her to join him. "Sorry for stomping off earlier. I just needed some time alone. To think."

Zoey made her way to the boulder and pulled herself up to sit next to him. "I understand. I'm sorry for coming after you, but it seemed like you'd been gone forever. I just wanted to make sure you were okay."

"I'll be fine," Spencer said, though the look on his face told Zoey he might not be. "At least I'm not going through what you and Andy are. I grew up in this world. You guys didn't. A lot was dropped on you in the last few days, and I'm sorry about that. I wish it didn't have to be this way."

Zoey tugged one of her tangled curls. "Honestly, I think Andy took it way worse than I did. I'm not sure he'd even still be coming with us if it weren't for the Fates telling him he might get his family back. But me . . . I mean, I feel guilty for this, but I watched my mom *die*. At least, I watched her as she was dying. And I'm not as upset as I think I should be." Her eyes filled with tears. "I hated that city. I hated almost everyone who lived there. None of them cared to ask what you were going through, or why you did the things you did. They just tormented you. I won't miss any of them. But at the same time, being relieved everyone is gone doesn't feel that great."

Spencer raised his eyebrows and leaned so close to her their shoulders touched. Warm tingles rushed through her body. "That place sounds terrible. But I understand how you feel . . . I don't think I'll miss anyone on Olympus. At least not anyone who's alive."

Zoey wiped her eyes. "Can I ask you something?" He nodded. "My dad—he—he abandoned me. And as much as I always try to forget him, I can't. I know I'll never get the closure I need, but I thought maybe, if I saw how he died, I'd get a glimpse into his life and . . ."

Spencer's eyes widened. "You want me to use my powers to show you how your father died?"

"Could you?" Zoey said.

Spencer looked away. "I'm not sure that's the best idea."

Zoey hugged her knees. "That's okay. It would probably hurt me more than anything. I don't even know why I asked."

"Because you still love him," Spencer said. "He abandoned you, but you still love him. And my visions would be your only chance to see him one last time, even if it meant you had to watch him die."

Zoey's jaw dropped. "How . . . What . . ."

"That's how I am about my dad, too." He forced another smile, his eyes sad, as if recalling a joyful memory that now brought pain.

"Your dad abandoned you?" Zoey said. "But I thought you grew up in Hades."

"I did, for a while. But, like the Fates said, demigods can't live outside Olympus forever. At age ten Zeus recruits us, and we have to live in his palace with him."

"And you didn't want to?"

Spencer shook his head. "My father can only leave Hades twice a year, on the winter and summer solstices. Those were the only times I'd get to see him, and for just a few minutes, if I lived on Olympus. I loved him more than anything. He and Persephone were my whole world, especially because my mother died right after I was born. I couldn't bear the thought of being away from them. But he let Zeus take me away. He thought he had to because of the prophecy."

"That's awful."

"Yeah. Syrena went through just about the same thing. Her dad lives in his undersea palace, and unless Zeus summons him for an Olympian meeting or it's the winter or summer solstice, he can't leave. That's part of the reason we became so close, I think. We knew exactly how the other felt."

Zoey's heart sank. "I'm sorry you lost someone so important to you."

Spencer's eyes grew watery, and he let out a cold laugh. "Yeah, well. That's love for you. It'll mess you up like crazy."

Zoey nodded. She'd been in love once, or at least what she *thought* was love at the time. With Jet Weaver. She'd trusted and cared for him enough to not only sleep with him, but also confide in him about her deepest, darkest secret—what she'd resorted to doing at age fourteen to pay her mother's apartment rent so they wouldn't be kicked into the streets—and he'd told everyone in school. She'd been tormented by her classmates ever since.

She hung her head, not wanting to think about his betrayal and the guilt she still harbored for what she'd done to make some quick money. "I know what you mean. Sometimes it's better to be alone."

Spencer shrugged. "I thought I'd be with Syrena forever. Now I don't know what the future holds for me."

Zoey wasn't sure how to reply, and they fell into awkward silence. A few minutes passed, and she sighed. "Do you think that even with Persephone's help, we'll have to face your father?"

Spencer cleared his throat and pulled himself to his feet. "If we make it to Hades on time and everything works out, we won't have to worry about facing him, I promise you. Persephone will make sure of it." He jumped off the boulder. "We'd better head back. I'm exhausted, and you need some serious rest after everything that's happened today. We have a lot of ground to cover tomorrow."

She climbed to her feet, ready to follow Spencer back to camp. The trees behind rustled, and she swung around, catching a glimpse of a young man in flight, his glowing gold eyes illuminating the scar on his face.

Spencer clenched his jaw. "Karter, what are you doing here?"

"I've come to save you from yourself, my friend," Karter said, landing before them.

"Quit following us," Zoey said, brandishing her axe and trying to mask her fear.

Karter turned to her, his eyes flashing under the light of the moon. His stare struck terror through her body. "You again."

"Leave her alone," Spencer said, and pulled his dagger from his robes. Karter took a step back, his eyes fixed on the knife.

Spencer lunged for Karter. He tackled him to the

ground and brought the blade of the dagger over his throat. Karter shoved Spencer away and jumped up. He conjured a gold lightning bolt, but Spencer hopped to his feet and punched Karter in the cheek. Karter stumbled to the side. Spencer kicked him in the stomach, then sent a fist flying into his temple.

Karter gasped for breath, stumbling to the forest floor. Spencer twirled the knife in his fingers, then plunged it into Karter's side. With a gut-wrenching *slice*, Spencer pulled it out. Karter coughed up blood. It painted the grass at his sandaled feet scarlet.

"We have to get back to camp," Zoey said, jumping to the ground, her heart in her throat. "We have to get out of here."

Spencer swung around, a crazed look in his dark eyes. For a moment Zoey thought he might stab her next. His nostrils flared. He shot Karter a glare. Karter clutched his side, blood pooling around him. "Spencer, please," he choked. "Don't do this."

"Let's go," Spencer replied, shaking his head. Zoey took his hand, and they ran from the scene.

CHAPTER EIGHT

SCAR

Screaming. It surrounded Karter, deafening and spine tingling.
But this time it wasn't Syrena.

It was Spencer.

Karter bolted through darkness, unable to see a thing, an electric
shock buzzing behind his ribs. He clawed his side and grabbed the
hilt of a knife, then tore it from his body. The wound throbbed with
hot pain. Sticky blood coated his clothes.

"Karter!" Spencer screamed. "Help me!"

Karter saw him not too far ahead, a ray of white light shining
down on him. He struggled against the same chains as Syrena, iron
chains bolted to the ground, shackled around his wrists and ankles.
"Please, my friend, save me."

Karter ran to him, determined to break the chains apart this
time, to save him. But before Karter even reached his side, Spencer
let out a scream so terrible it sent shudders through Karter's body.
The blade of a sword had been thrust through Spencer's chest from
behind. An invisible force ripped it back out.

Tears filled Karter's eyes, and he grabbed the chains. He tried to pry them apart, Spencer's blood spilling over his hands. But they wouldn't break. He wasn't strong enough. "No!" Karter cried. "No no no no!" Spencer slipped to the ground, his eyes glazing over. Karter sobbed and cradled Spencer's head in his lap.

As Karter cried, he looked up at the darkness, more hopeless than ever. "Please, if there's someone out there listening, someone who cares, I'm begging you to help me."

A strangely familiar woman's voice said, "There, there. You'll be just fine, Son of Zeus." A million sparkling stars appeared in an instant, dancing around Karter and engulfing him with blissful warmth.

Karter gasped, and his eyes fluttered open.

Wait, what had happened—

He'd been going west, like the voice told him. He'd been trying to find Spencer. He'd found him— Spencer stabbed him—

But what happened after that?

He sat up, surprised to find himself in a tiny cave. Moonlight poked through the entrance, the tranquil whisper of a stream outside. He blinked a few times, trying to clear his vision, and caught a glimpse of red hair and a glittering dress. He squinted, focusing, then realized it was Asteria, the Titan goddess, staring back at him with her head cocked to one side like a curious puppy.

He shot into the air and knocked his head on the ceiling. "Ow! What— You— Titan!"

Asteria crossed her arms. "That's the kind of thank-you I get for saving your life?"

He paused and fell to the floor of the cave, then pressed his fingers where he'd been stabbed. There was nothing. No pain. He peered down his robes to find his skin undamaged.

Asteria really had saved his life, but how? She wasn't a goddess of medicine or healing. He cleared his throat. Despite what the gods said, if she was willing to save his life, perhaps she was someone he could trust. "Thank you for—for saving my life."

Her eyes softened, her lips curling into a gentle smile. "You're welcome, Son of Zeus."

"But I'm confused. How did you do it? Healing isn't in the realm of your power."

"You're right. But one god of healing in particular has owed me a favor for thousands of years, and although you're trying to capture his daughter, he agreed to heal you when I asked."

Karter raised an eyebrow. "Apollo? Well, of course he agreed. Diana is a traitor and should be brought to justice."

Asteria chuckled. "Not every god is so black and white."

"Why did Apollo owe *you* a favor?"

"Oh, it was a long time ago. Your father pursued me after the Titan War, and I leapt into the sea and turned myself into the island of Delos. Later he and my sister, Leto, formed a—*relationship* behind lovely Hera's back, and you know how *she* is. Always so jealous of her husband's conquests. Soon Leto became pregnant with Apollo and

Artemis. Of course Hera found out and, being a goddess of many things, including childbirth, made it so Leto could not give birth on any mainland, any island of the sea, or any place under the sun. But because I was not a natural island, my sister was able to give birth on me, and after Apollo was born, he thanked me and asked if I wished for a favor in return. I told him that if something should arise, I would summon him."

Karter brushed the shaggy locks from his eyes. "Why did you use the favor on me? It doesn't make any sense."

Asteria took his hand. Her skin was soft, warm. "I am a goddess of prophetic dreams, Son of Zeus. And I have seen the greatness you are destined to achieve."

Karter knit his brow. "But I've already achieved greatness. I'm a warrior of the gods, one of the strongest demigods of my generation. What more can I do, other than achieve immortality like my brother Heracles?"

Asteria smiled. "You must continue following the Son of Hades to find out."

Karter pulled away. "How can I? He just tried to kill me. As much as I want to get him back, there's no changing him now."

She shook her head. "You're wrong. You *must* continue to try." He turned away and brushed his scar, looking outside at the blinking stars. "You're scared," she said. "You're scared Zeus might punish you again."

Karter stood and glared down at her. "I've already risked everything for Spencer. If my father finds out what's happened—"

"He won't. Not yet. Not while you still have a chance to save your friend."

Karter paused and ran his hands through his hair. If a goddess of prophecy really thought there was a way to save Spencer, if she really thought this was the way to achieve his destined greatness, shouldn't he listen to her? She'd used her favor from Apollo to save his life. Shouldn't he trust her?

He sighed, his scar throbbing with the memory of old pain. "All right. I'll go after him."

"You must go west."

Six years ago . . .

Fall, Year 494 AS

The halls of the Olympian palace were lined with marble statues of gods, and the golden tiled floor shimmered from the blinding sunlight pouring in through wide, arched windows. Someone, probably Apollo, played a soft tune on a lyre a few halls down, and Karter hummed along as he made his way to Spencer's bedroom.

He reached the door, a barrier with skulls and bones carved into the wood. He knocked and waited.

No answer.

He tugged the handle, and the door opened.

The tall, dark, windowless walls swallowed Karter as he

walked inside, the tile floor cold on his bare feet. Spencer's bed, the only piece of furniture, was pushed up against the far wall, a solid black canopy curtained around it.

The familiar voice of a girl whispered something incomprehensible from behind the canopy, and Karter crossed his arms, smirking. Syrena must be visiting Spencer. Again.

"Did you guys ignore the knock on the door, or were you too involved with each other to hear it?" Karter said, laughing.

The whispering stopped, and the canopy was pulled away. Spencer and Syrena emerged from the shadows. Their robes were wrinkled, their cheeks flushed. "We weren't doing anything weird, if that's what you mean," Spencer said.

Syrena elbowed his arm. "We were just discussing something important."

Karter raised an eyebrow. "Yeah? And what's that?"

"We want to visit our fathers," Syrena said.

Karter's jaw dropped. "Wait, what? But—you can't leave Olympus. Not without a mission assigned to you by my father. Did he say you could go?"

"No," Spencer said. "We planned to just—you know, sneak out."

Karter rushed toward them, panic brewing in his chest. Spencer was only fourteen, Syrena thirteen. They were so young, and obviously not thinking clearly. Karter was sixteen, the big brother of the group. Perhaps he could talk some sense into them. "You can't do that. If my father finds out— I mean, he's *killed* demigods for lesser offenses."

Syrena put her hands on her hips and rolled her eyes. "Maybe so. But the worst he'd do to us is give us a few lashings. We are some of his most powerful demigods, after all."

Karter grabbed their shoulders. "It doesn't matter. He's in charge. He's not just a god—he's *king* of the gods. Ruler of the planet. You can't go. You can't break his rules. Just try to see your fathers at the winter solstice party coming up."

They pulled away from his grasp. "Easy for you to say," Spencer said. "You get to see Zeus more than once or twice a year. You live in his palace. You don't go through what we do every day."

Karter bit his lip. "I'll never see my mother again."

Syrena scoffed. "At least you *knew* your mother. Both of ours died before we were even old enough to meet them."

Karter balled his fists, his chest tight with buried fury. He wanted to scream at them for downplaying the very real pain he went through regarding his mother, but knew if he lost his cool it would push them even more to sneak out. He jabbed a finger at their noses. "You two better not sneak away. This is my only warning. If you try, my father will figure it out. And I don't know what terrible things he'll do to you." With that, Karter stormed out of the bedroom, praying his words would change their minds.

A few days passed, and to Karter's relief, he'd heard nothing from Spencer and Syrena about sneaking away from Olympus to see their fathers.

It was nighttime, and Karter planned to meet his girl-friend, Violet, Daughter of Aphrodite, for a romantic walk in the Garden of Olympus—the place they always held their dates.

He stood before a body-length mirror hanging from one of the walls of his bedroom, staring at his handsome reflection. At his light-brown eyes, at his perfect complexion. He ruffled his hair, then left to meet Violet.

He reached the garden, half the size of the Olympian palace. Along the outer edge and scattered throughout, cypress trees stood a hundred feet tall. Bushes with wide varieties of flowers were planted there, which created a rainbow of color, a multitude of shapes to draw one's hungry eyes, and a dizzying mix of delicious, potent fragrances. Water danced through marble fountains into ponds, where arrays of exotic fish splashed.

As Karter began his walk along the shiny paths to meet her, trumpets blared in alarm from the palace. His stomach sank, dread overcoming him. He leapt into the air and flew back as fast as he could.

When he reached the palace, he spotted Athena walking hastily down the halls. She was tall and beautiful, her silver curls piled atop her head in an elegant bun, her dress billowing behind her.

"Athena, what's going on?" he said.

She swung around to look at him, her expression full of worry. "The Olympians have been summoned to the throne room. Some demigods tried to escape."

Karter shook his head in disbelief and flew ahead of her. She cried for him to stop.

He reached the huge, empty throne room. Its curved white walls were lined with sleek thrones and marble pillars with swirls winding all the way up. The shooting stars and constellations from the pitch-black ceiling gleamed down at him, fluffy clouds floating aimlessly in the dark outside the arched windows.

Footsteps sounded from behind, and he hid behind the nearest throne, watching the entrance as a few of the Olympian gods shuffled inside. They dragged Spencer and Syrena by iron chains shackled around their wrists and ankles. Karter's jaw dropped, his heart racing with panic.

The gods took their seats, and Karter peered around the other side of the throne to watch the scene.

Once everyone was situated, a cruel laugh rang through the air. Hera's laugh. She gave Spencer and Syrena a sinister smile, swinging her thick braid over her shoulders. She tapped her polished fingernails on the armrest of her throne. "We should kill them immediately."

Apollo, with his curly strawberry-blond hair and tanned skin, all swathed in radiant light, frowned at her. "What's wrong with you, Hera? They're some of our most powerful demigods, and this is their first offense. Why would we kill them?"

Hera pointed one long, slim finger at Apollo. "They need to be punished with the utmost severity for their crimes. We cannot allow them to get away with treason."

Apollo laughed. "I'm sure you wouldn't feel that way if they were born inside wedlock."

Artemis threw her hands in the air, her long curls a frizzy mess. "For once, I agree with Hera. We must set an example for the other demigods. They cannot come and go as they please."

"I'm surprised at you, sister," Apollo said.

Aphrodite fluffed her hair and batted her eyes. "Will no one ask why they tried to escape? Perhaps they have good reason for what they've done."

Ares chortled, his red face growing even brighter than usual. "I love you dearly, Aphrodite, but I do believe you're missing the point Hera and Artemis have made."

Before Aphrodite could snap back, there was a clap of thunder, and the clouds outside turned dark. The gods quieted, all of them looking to Karter's father. Karter trembled.

His father stroked his beard, fixing his eyes on Spencer and Syrena. "They are too valuable to kill, and so we will not." Karter let out a quiet sigh of relief. "But they will be punished severely." Karter's heart leapt into his throat. Punished severely? No matter how stupid a decision they'd made, the thought of his two best friends being tortured was enough to make his stomach sick.

"And how do you propose we punish them, husband?" Hera said.

"With lightning," his father said.

Karter bolted out from behind the throne and fell at his father's feet. "No!" he cried. "Please, don't hurt them!" The Olympians let out a collective gasp, then burst into gossipy whispers. Athena stared down at Karter with a furrowed brow.

Karter's father narrowed his eyes. "What is the meaning of this? Only the Olympian gods are permitted to be here."

Hera glared down at Karter. "Do not argue with Zeus's ruling. He has shown mercy to your friends. If I had it my way, they would already be dead."

"If you had it your way, everyone would be dead," Apollo said.

Karter bowed. "Don't hurt them. They won't try to escape again. I'll make sure of it."

Miniature lightning bolts hissed around his father's head. "So, my son, you take responsibility for their crimes?"

"Yes, Father. Yes," Karter said.

"Then stand." Karter did as he was told. "Because you accept their crimes as your own, you will take their punishment." His stomach dropped. "For your blatant disrespect for my ruling, and for disregarding orders, your punishment will be increased tenfold."

Hera cackled. "Will he die, then?"

"No," his father said. "He's an important pawn of the

game. *My* game. We cannot kill him. But he will learn respect today."

Karter's eyes filled with tears. He fell to his knees. "Father, I know respect."

Syrena began to sob. Spencer grew pale. "Don't do this. Syrena and I—we're the ones who deserve the punishment. Not Karter."

Karter's father rose. He conjured a gold lightning bolt. "It's too late now. My son has decided the outcome." He raised the bolt, and Karter closed his eyes.

Pain hotter than the flames of Tartarus seared his face.

CHAPTER NINE

STONE

Now . . .

Andy woke with a start to Zoey shaking him, the sky still dark. "Wake up, Andy! Wake up! We have to go!"

He sat up groggily and grabbed his sword. "Is there a monster? What's going on?"

"We were attacked by that scar-faced guy, Karter. Spencer . . . took care of him, but we need to go. In case he manages to follow us."

Andy scrambled to his feet. The group gathered their things, put out what was left of the campfire, and raced into the trees.

They ran until they couldn't anymore, then slowed to a fast walk. The sun rose, but they pressed on, fleeing until late afternoon. By that time, they agreed they needed to eat something and stopped for lunch. Once they ate, they decided it was better to walk for the rest of the day rather than sleep. Andy's whole body was sore and he was beyond exhausted, just like everyone else, but a little pain and sleepiness was better than being attacked by an angry, scar-faced demigod.

Andy fell a bit behind the group, trying to keep his eyes open, his head bobbing up and down. He crossed his arms, glaring tiredly at Zoey and Spencer as they walked side by side. They talked as though they'd been friends forever, which was strange, because they'd only known each other for a little over two days. It wasn't much longer than Andy had known Zoey, but still. The sight of them made him want to gag.

Diana looked over her shoulder at Andy, dark, puffy bags under her bloodshot eyes. She smirked. "You don't look very happy." She jerked her head in Zoey and Spencer's direction.

Andy's cheeks grew hot. "Shut up."

Even after all the crying Diana had done the night before, and even though she hadn't slept in over twenty-four hours, a mischievous smile formed on her lips. He raised an eyebrow at her. She gave him a wink, then hopped ahead and wiggled between Zoey and Spencer. She laced her arm with Spencer's and pulled him along.

Zoey's face fell as if someone had stolen the last slice of pizza she wanted. Andy caught up to her. He nudged her shoulder with his own. "Hey, uh, you."

She looked over and gave him a halfhearted smile. "Hey."

Andy's palms began to sweat. He nibbled on the tip of

his thumb. "Uh . . . How are, uh, you?"

"Tired. Achy. But I think we all are. It's been one hell of an adventure so far. How're you?"

Andy shoved his hands into his sweatshirt pocket and looked up at the trees. "Well, I mean, considering all that's happened, and the fact you're here with me . . . I mean, what I'm trying to say is . . ." But he wasn't sure what he was trying to say. He just wanted a reason to talk to her. To occupy her attention.

She didn't try to keep the conversation going. Instead, she looked ahead, and they walked alongside each other in disappointing silence.

For the rest of the afternoon, they didn't see any monsters. They did, however, see tons of woodland creatures, most notably a pack of wolves with silver fur. The sight had startled Andy, but even more shocking was the fact that the wolves seemed to be intimidated by the group, as if they knew who they were and not to mess with them. They put their tails between their legs, ears down, and ran off before Andy could even draw his sword.

When the sun began to set that evening, it was time to train again. There wasn't a clearing nearby, so they settled for a spot less dense with forest next to a clear stream. Andy and Zoey seated themselves on the log of a fallen tree. Diana prepared their camp for the night, and Spencer knelt before them and pressed his thumbs to their foreheads.

Again, fog consumed Andy. He was beginning to

grow accustomed to barreling through the darkness, so he didn't scream this time. Rather, he waited patiently to be immersed in a new scene encompassing death. He prayed Spencer's plan would work, that they'd both absorb the knowledge of battle and come out stronger for it. But most of all, he prayed all of this would help him get his family back.

Suddenly he found himself running down streets of Apollo City, toward the temple, accompanied by Syrena, Karter, and a second team of demigod warriors. There was a riot at the temple. Hostages had been taken, and tons of citizens had already been killed. Many of the satyr and centaur *astynomia*, the order keepers of the cities, had also been murdered. Apollo had wanted to stop the rioters himself, but Zeus decided it would be better if he sent two of his best demigod teams to kill them and save the rest of the citizens, to test their strength as heroes.

The remaining *astynomia* were ordered to pull back their efforts, and the demigods were sent in.

Hundreds of houses and shops, big and small, surrounded Andy. The golden sun blazed high in a cloudless blue sky. Bruised and battered people that must have escaped the rioters' clutches ran, screaming, along the cobblestone paths away from the white-pillared Temple of Apollo. It was so tall it nearly reached the sky, so wide it could encompass several houses. Fierce cries issued from inside.

The demigods darted between screaming people, sandaled feet pounding against the path, weapons drawn. *We'll send those criminals straight to Tartarus!* Andy thought. In the last couple of years, he'd grown used to taking lives on missions similar to this.

They ran up the steps, past the pillars, and through the entryway of the temple. Carved in the ceiling was an image of Apollo as he drove his fiery chariot across the sky, pulling the sun behind him. Dead bodies of citizens were scattered across the floor. Sunlight flooded through the windows, shining on the marble statues of a naked Apollo in different poses that had been knocked to the stone floor.

In the center, fifty to sixty men and women stood together, various weapons in hand, clothes torn and bloody. A few people lay tied up and unconscious behind them.

"The *astynomia* said demigods would be coming," one man said, raising a sword. "We'll kill you all with pleasure."

Karter stepped forward. He'd always been a leader among the demigods. "Why are you doing this? Why are you hurting people? It didn't have to be this way. You could have lived long, productive lives here in the city. But now you have to die."

A woman spat in Karter's direction. "We grow tired of being controlled by the gods. We want our freedom. And we'll do whatever it takes to get it." The rest of the men and women yelled in agreement. They raised their weapons and, together, they charged.

Andy snarled and lunged for them. Within seconds, his

spear impaled five of them, one by one. He pounded his shield against ten others' temples. They crumpled to the floor.

To Andy's right, Karter blasted criminals into the walls and ceiling with gold lightning bolts. Syrena whipped their weapons away with her water, then sent daggers through their hearts. To his left, Diana, the Daughter of Apollo, a member of the second team of demigod warriors, blasted their heads into chunks of bone and brain with spheres of light. Her teammates—Pearl, another Daughter of Poseidon and Syrena's younger, beloved half-sister, and Layla, a Daughter of Ares—chopped them to bits with their swords.

Six more advanced on Andy. Four jabbed their spears at him, but he blocked the attacks with the shaft of his spear, then sliced their throats in perfect sequence. The last two came at him, hacking the air with their weapons, but Andy threw up his shield and shoved them backward. He sent his spear through one's stomach, ripped it out, then shoved it through the second's.

Diana let out a cry of horror to Andy's left. He looked over, and his heart stopped, his breath caught in his throat.

At Diana's feet, Pearl's head lay, the rest of her body mangled on the side. Blood pooled around the stump of her neck, staining her choppy silver hair a deep shade of red. Her eyes, the color of ocean waves, usually so vibrant, were lifeless.

Diana dropped to her knees. Her trembling hands

glowed with golden light. She reached for Pearl's cheeks. "No, no, no. Pearl."

A few feet away from Diana, a woman clutching a bloody axe smiled. "She won't be the last to die today." She stomped toward Diana. Andy was about to step in, but before he could even move, Layla jumped in front of Diana to fight the woman.

Layla's face contorted with fury as she swung her sword and blocked the woman's attacks. Her skin and eyes, both a deep-brown shade, shifted into an angry red. The burgundy coils piled atop her head seemed to stand up straight. She kicked the woman to the ground and plunged the sword's blade through her neck. The woman's head fell to the floor. Layla let out a shrill cry, then charged for the rest of the rioters—there were maybe ten left—with more anger than even her father, the God of War himself.

Syrena rushed to Diana's side. Diana held Pearl's head near the rest of the body, and her hands glowed bright, her eyes closed in concentration. Sobs racked Syrena's body. "My sister!" she wailed.

Andy snarled, hot rage flooding his chest at the sight of Pearl, and at the sight of Syrena's tears. He and Karter dashed to Layla's side. Together, they killed the last of the rioters. Layla cut them to pieces, Karter bashed their skulls in, and Andy impaled them.

Once finished, they rushed toward Diana, Syrena, and Pearl.

The light in Diana's hands faded, but Pearl was still

sliced in two. An eerie silence filled the temple. They'd succeeded in their mission for Zeus; all they had to do now was free the unconscious hostages and restore what had been destroyed in the temple and city during the riots. But they'd lost a fellow demigod in the process.

The smell of sweat and urine stung Andy's nostrils. He hung his head. Pearl was a sweet girl, adored by all, but especially by Syrena and Diana.

Syrena cared for her for obvious reasons: she was her sister, the only other living demigod child of Poseidon close to her age. They'd spent many days together playing in the ocean they'd once called home.

But Diana loved her in a different way. Diana loved her the way Andy did Syrena, and Pearl had reciprocated those feelings.

Diana's whole body shook. Tears rolled down her cheeks. "I couldn't heal her. Why couldn't I heal her?" She exhaled, and clouds of smoke floated from her lips.

"Diana, are you okay?" Karter asked, reaching for her.

She whipped around, giving Karter a glare that sent chills through Andy's body. Her hair erupted with yellow fire, and flames shot from her eyes. "No!" she roared.

"Diana!" Layla cried, rushing toward her.

Fog crept into the corners of Andy's vision. The last thing he saw before it consumed him was Diana as her body lit with flames. She exploded in a violent flash of golden light.

The fog cleared. Andy was back in the forest. Spencer pulled away from him and Zoey, sweat dripping down his forehead. He gasped for breath, and Andy thought he caught a glimpse of tears in Spencer's eyes. "I'm so sorry," Spencer said. "I tried to stop the vision before—before you'd see Pearl, but it got away from me. That's not something I like to remember, but I thought that battle would help you a lot."

Andy gritted his teeth, his nostrils flaring as he tried to catch his breath. He was getting used to the disorientation he felt when he returned from the visions, but it still jarred him.

He darted his gaze around the camp, trying to spot Diana. He'd only known her for three days, but after witnessing *that* vision, he had the very strong urge to give her a hug.

She stood a ways away, arms crossed, watching them with sad, droopy eyes. "You showed them the fight with Pearl?"

Zoey gulped. "Yeah. Was that the first time you . . . you know, discovered your big bad sunlight powers? The time you almost died?"

Diana sighed, made her way to Andy's side, and sat down cross-legged. "Yes. I nearly killed everyone left in the temple, including myself. Thankfully my father was watching over our mission, and he healed us.

"He didn't like the fact that Zeus had us handling it all by ourselves when it was happening in his city. He's always been overprotective of me." She closed her eyes tight.

"After that day, Syrena and I became best friends, while Layla and I drifted apart. Syrena and I blamed the gods for Pearl's death, but she didn't. I never did understand why she kept defending them. If Zeus hadn't been testing us in such a reckless way, Pearl would still be here. Plus, they had all the power to bring her back to life, which granted, would have made her an immortal god, so I understand why they didn't do it, but still, they could have.

"Pretty soon Syrena and I started to blame the gods for everything else, too, because they're awful, and that's why we decided to bring the prophecy to fruition." She opened her eyes and smiled. "If you guys are able to win this war, no one else will have to pointlessly suffer at the gods' hands."

Andy felt as if someone were crushing his lungs. Being told he was part of a prophecy that would determine the fate of the world was already more than enough pressure, but Diana had just made it really, *really* personal.

Although the group was exhausted, for the rest of the evening until dinner, they sparred. Andy and Zoey made steady progress, both of them able to stand their ground against the demigods for almost a minute despite their tiredness. Andy noticed that each time Spencer so much as smiled at Zoey, she blushed. He spent most of the night rolling his eyes and wanting to puke.

Diana and Spencer agreed to watch for monsters in shifts—that way they'd both get some sleep—and the moment Andy's head hit the grass, he was out.

As the group trudged on early the next morning, they reached a small clearing with periwinkle bellflowers growing between bushes and tall grass. Diana and Spencer stopped and drew their weapons. Someone was in the shadows of the trees at the edge of the clearing. An unmoving, silent dark outline.

Andy drew his sword. Zoey raised her axe. They approached the being, but as they grew closer, Andy lowered his weapon. It wasn't dangerous. In fact, it wasn't even alive.

It was a statue carved from stone of a man who couldn't be older than twenty. Curved horns came out of his head, the bottom half of his body a hooved barnyard animal. He held up a sword. A look of terror was etched on his face.

"Oh. My. Gods," Diana whispered.

Zoey reached out and touched the statue. "What's wrong? He can't hurt us. He's not real."

Spencer glared at the trees ahead. "No, he can't. But what did this to him . . ."

The realization hit Andy like a bus going ninety miles an hour. "It was Medusa, wasn't it?" He turned to Zoey. "Medusa is a monster, and if you look into her eyes you turn to stone."

Zoey's eyes widened. She pulled away from the statue. "What the hell."

Spencer shook his head. "How did a satyr get all the way out here, though?"

Diana drew her bow. "I heard a few escapee satyrs had a village someplace west. Maybe he's from there."

"Or maybe he was trying to get there," Spencer said.

"So he's a satyr?" Andy said. "I'm guessing that's a creature that's half man, half donkey? I think I remember them from the myths I've heard about."

Diana shot him a glare. "Satyrs are half man, half *goat*," she corrected. "In the old days they just drank as much alcohol as possible and chased pretty nymphs around. But now they act as *astynomia*, the ones who keep order and enforce the laws in the twelve cities." She jerked her head toward the statue. "And they're clearly *not* a myth."

Andy shrugged. "All right. Noted."

Above, Andy heard a loud *whoosh*, then the sound of a dart hitting a board. He swung around to see an arrow had impaled the branch of a tree behind them, its wooden body and feathered tail quivering.

Ahead of them, the voice of a boy said, "Get away from my brother."

Clopping toward them through the trees was a scrawny satyr who couldn't have been older than thirteen. His cherry-black hair hung in waves over his hooded brown eyes and matched the fur of his legs. His skin was deeply tanned. He held a bow and arrow with shaking hands, his expression full of fear.

Diana leapt toward him, bow drawn. "Get back."

The satyr halted, nearly tripping over his hooves. "Who are you?" His voice cracked with traces of puberty.

"My brother. You're standing by my brother."

Diana gestured toward the stone satyr. "Is that who you're talking about? Sorry to break it to you, kid, but he's dead."

"I know," the satyr said, his eyes welling with tears. He dropped his weapon. "Medusa—she—she killed him."

Diana lowered her bow. "When did that happen? Is she close?"

The satyr wiped his tears. "It happened yesterday, and I think she is. I'm looking for her."

Andy stepped forward. "Looking for her? Why? Why don't you go home? You shouldn't be out here all by yourself."

"I can't go home," the satyr replied, bursting into a fit of sobs. "My brother and I, we escaped our city. We planned to go to Alikan Village. That's where satyrs go when they leave the cities. But Phoenix was the one who knew where to go. Phoenix was the one who took care of everything." He picked up his bow and arrow and stuffed them into the pack slung over his back. "I'm going to find Medusa, and I'm going to kill her for what she did to him."

"But you're just a kid," Zoey said. "You plan to kill her all by yourself?"

He hung his head. "I have to."

Andy and Zoey exchanged a knowing glance, and Andy made his way to the satyr's side. He rested a hand on his shoulder. "You can't do it alone."

Zoey smiled. "We can help you slay her. And after we

finish our own mission, we'll help you find Alikan Village."
The satyr's face lit up, and he dried his tears.

Spencer stepped forward, his dark eyes stern. "We only
have a week to get to Hades. We can't stray from our mission." He turned toward the satyr. "I'm sorry you lost your
brother, but we can't help you."

The satyr frowned, and Andy's chest tightened in frustration. He understood they were on a strict time schedule,
but the kid just lost his brother. "He needs help," Andy
said. "Just like Vanessa did. We can't abandon people in
need."

"I'm not sure you understand how dangerous Medusa
is," Diana said. "You look into her eyes once—I mean
once, even after she's dead—and you turn to stone. And
you don't come back."

Zoey put a hand on her hip. "Which is exactly why we
need to slay her. What if we kept her head and used it as
a weapon against more monsters we might come across?
What if we used it against the gods? It would make things
a lot easier."

Spencer frowned. "When the gods brought Medusa
back to life, they made it so she couldn't turn immortals to
stone any longer. It would be useless against them."

"What about monsters, though?" Zoey said.

"Yeah, it would work on monsters," Spencer said. "But
still, it's dangerous, and not something we should risk our
lives for. Our job is to get to Hades and steal the Helm of
Darkness. This isn't our problem." The satyr averted his

gaze to his hooves.

Zoey shot Spencer a bewildered look. "How can you say that?"

Spencer opened his mouth to reply, but Andy beat him to it, his face hot with anger. "This kid's brother just died. How many people have to die at the hands of monsters before you start to care?"

"I do care," Spencer said. "But I'm telling you, this isn't a good idea."

Andy sighed. "Look, I don't care what you say. I'm helping this kid. I'm helping him kill Medusa, and I'm helping him find the village."

Spencer threw his hands in the air. "You've got to be joking. You just started your training. You can't last a minute against Diana and me, let alone Medusa. Besides, how do you think you're going to find her, or Alikan Village? This forest is huge. You'd be wasting your time."

"It's not a waste of time," Zoey snapped. "If we have her head, it would make the rest of our mission infinitely easier. If we'd had her head when the Stymphalian Birds attacked, no one would have gotten hurt. That little girl would still be alive, and so would Penny and Maia."

Spencer glared at Zoey. "If you do this, both of you could die. You'll be risking everything. If you fail, Syrena will have died for nothing."

"Maybe so," Zoey said. "But if we're supposed to go into the underworld within the next week, and possibly face off with one of the strongest gods in all of existence, we should be able to slay one measly monster. And if we can't, well, then maybe we weren't worthy of this quest, and maybe she would have died for nothing anyway."

Spencer let out a cold laugh. "I'm not taking you to Medusa. I'm not helping you kill yourselves." Zoey's face fell.

Andy jabbed his finger in Spencer's face. "That's your own choice. But I'm not standing by and letting this kid face Medusa alone. We've already decided what we're going to do, so you can either come with, or we can leave you behind."

"And what about your family?" Spencer said. "What if you die fighting her, and because of it, you never get the chance to see them again?"

Andy sucked in a sharp breath. Spencer brought up a good point—what about his family? His best friend? If he died, he'd never make it to Hades. He'd never get the chance to save them. A heavy ache weighed in his chest. "I think that—that I won't have to worry about it." He balled his fists. "No, I *know* I won't, because we can take on Medusa. We can slay her. We're ready." He wasn't sure of his own words, but he planned to stick by them.

Spencer glared in silence at Andy, but Andy refused to give in. He glared back, his eyes burning.

Diana rested a hand on Spencer's shoulder. "I know there's a huge chance they could fail, but we can't make them do something, or rather, *not* do something. They're their own people, and they've spoken. All we can do is help them and make sure no one gets hurt."

Spencer looked away. "Fine. We'll try to kill Medusa. And if by some stroke of luck we succeed, I'll help you find Alikan Village after we get out of Hades."

The satyr thanked them and introduced himself as Darko. They introduced themselves as well, explaining their quest to fight the gods. By the time they finished, Darko's jaw had dropped, his eyes shining with awe.

They began the search for Medusa, trying their best to hurry.

"So why were you and your brother all the way out here, Darko?" Zoey asked as they pressed on through the forest.

Darko bit his nails, and Andy smiled, reminded of his own nervous habits. "I was being trained to become part of the *astynomia* in Hermes City. My brother, Phoenix, he hated the job. It's more like slavery, really. It's dangerous, restrictive . . . You don't have a say in how your life goes." He dropped his hands to his sides. "Phoenix didn't want that kind of life for us. He'd heard of a village farther west in the country, from a kind of underground association, and we escaped the city. I don't know how long we'd been looking for Alikan Village, but it seemed like years. All I wanted was to get there, to be safe from the gods and monsters. But then Medusa went and took my brother away from me." His eyes filled with tears, and Andy rested a hand on his shoulder. He hoped the gesture would bring Darko some comfort.

"How did you escape her?" Zoey asked.

Darko wiped his eyes. "Phoenix screamed. I saw his legs turn to stone, and then his hands. I heard her laugh—it was the creepiest thing—and I ran. I've never run away from someone so fast in my whole life." He clenched his jaw. "I wish I wasn't so scared of everything. I wish I hadn't run away. I wish I would have been brave enough to kill her when I had the chance."

"It's okay to be afraid sometimes," Zoey assured him. "And even though you ran away before, you're not now."

Even late into the afternoon, the group couldn't find any sign of the monster, or any more stone victims. Diana suggested she might be in a cave, but there were no caves in sight.

When the sun began to set, Diana and Spencer had Andy and Zoey train, and once it was dark outside, they decided to call it a night.

While Diana and Spencer prepared dinner, they lectured Andy and Zoey on how the hero named Perseus slayed Medusa in the old days.

"So that he could see her, he looked at her reflection in his shield," Diana said. "He chopped off her head and later used it to save the princess Andromeda from a huge sea monster."

When they went to sleep, Darko drifted off before anyone else, curled up close to the fire. Sadness overcame Andy as he watched the satyr yelp and twitch in his restless sleep, his face stretched in a grimace. He was probably having a nightmare.

The next day started just as uneventful as the afternoon and night before. The group searched and searched and searched the surrounding area, but still found nothing.

By late morning, however, they stumbled upon the entrance to a cave with two stone men frozen in terror just outside its jagged mouth. The cave was a monster ready to devour them, the black abyss of its throat waiting for them to slip inside and seal their fates.

Andy and Zoey exchanged a glance. "I think it's safe to say this is it," Zoey said. She gestured toward the statues. "I mean, considering, you know."

"She could have just been passing through," Andy said. "But there's only one way to know for sure."

Diana gathered two tree branches, ripped bits of cloth from her dress, and used them to construct torches. She lit them using her powers, then handed Spencer a torch, keeping one for herself. They all drew their weapons.

Spencer let out a heavy sigh and narrowed his eyes at the cave. "Let's go in."

They slipped into chilling darkness.

Pebbles littered the cave floor. Its long, wide caverns led on for what seemed like miles through echoing black chambers, stalactites hanging from the ceilings. Water dripped slow and steady, and somewhere beyond, creepy crawlies scurried.

Soon an eerie blue glow glimmered against the dark far ahead. They grew closer to the light, finding a tall, wide cavern infested with thousands of tiny blue glow worms strung across the walls and ceiling like Christmas lights, webs hanging over their heads like bits of shiny tinsel. They stepped into the new cavern, a pool of water soaking Andy's feet. As they continued through the cave, it seemed as though all the caverns were just like that one: glowing blue with bioluminescent bugs, water pooled on the floor.

Speckled gray statues began to pop up all over the caverns. There were men, satyrs, and even a mother shielding her daughter, all with terror etched on their faces. It made Andy's chest twist into an angry knot.

It seemed as if they'd been walking for hours in silence. "I don't think we're going to find her," Spencer said. "Are you sure you don't want to go back?"

Andy groaned. "Was that your plan all along? If it took a little too long, you'd try to convince us to turn back?"

Before Spencer could reply, the sound of hissing serpents reverberated ahead. A chill shot up Andy's spine. He scanned the caverns before them, but they were empty.

A laugh pierced through the hissing, echoing off the walls. A woman's, deep and husky. Malevolent, yet seductive at the same time.

"Ah, ah, ah," sang a voice that could only belong to the laughing woman. "Who-o has come to try and slay me this time?" She sniffed. "A satyr." More sniffing. "Two regular mortals. And two demigods. I've been blessed with de-helicious prey today."

Zoey waved her axe. "Who's there? Show yourself."

There was a blur of movement, and Andy caught a glimpse of black silk, green scales, and silver angel wings swooping down from the ceiling of a cavern far ahead.

"It's her," Spencer said. "Don't look into her eyes." Andy swung around, his heart in his throat, and stared only at the reflection of his shield, just as Perseus had done on his own quest.

Medusa was the most terrifying woman he'd ever seen, yet somehow, she was still beautiful. Her skin was made of scales like shimmering emeralds against the light of the glow worms. She wore a long silk dress that hugged her curvaceous body in all the right ways. Her cheekbones were sharp as daggers, and her pouty lips curled in a flirtatious smirk. Where her hair should have been, dozens of little snakes writhed and hissed. Feathered silver wings flapped behind her, attached to her shoulder blades.

Medusa smiled, her sharp teeth a dazzling white. She blew Andy a kiss through the reflection. "Ah, ah, it's been thousands of years since a man looked at me like *that*. All the rest claimed I was ugly. You-ou must have good taste in women." Andy said nothing, entranced with her strange reflection.

Spencer launched his spear into Medusa's shoulder. She wailed, a sound like millions of tiny glass shards shattering against a hardwood floor, her snakes standing up straight on her head. As she screamed, Andy snapped back to reality. He clutched his sword, ready to fight.

Medusa snarled and ripped the spear from her shoulder. Black fluid spat from her wound, and she brandished the weapon. "How rude." She raised it above her head. "Do I come into your house uninvited and throw spears at you?"

She chucked the spear straight for the group. Andy and Zoey somersaulted to the right. Darko clopped after them, and Spencer and Diana darted to the left. The spear clattered to the floor behind them.

Medusa clutched her chest and sighed, batting her eyelashes. "Ah, sweet young mortal." She stared into the reflection of Andy's shield and beckoned him with inviting arms. "Why don't you come closer? I like you. Don't you like me?"

Spencer threw a rock, and it bounced off her head. "I can't think of anyone who likes creepy gorgons, except maybe fat, ugly cyclopes. And still, that would be stooping pretty low."

Medusa growled and turned her attention to Spencer. She flapped her wings and flew straight for him, disappearing from the reflection of Andy's shield. He fumbled with it, catching sight of her again.

Spencer jumped out of Medusa's way, but she darted after him with incredible speed. She seized him by the shoulders before he could escape again, and he dropped his things, his torch going out as it fell into the cavern's pool. She pulled him into the air. Diana launched a sphere of light for Medusa's head, but she dodged the attack.

Spencer squirmed in Medusa's grasp, his eyes shut

tight. Her snakes danced around his face and flicked their tongues. "You will look into my eyes," she hissed. "You will turn to stone. You will die here."

Zoey turned toward Andy, hooking her axe to her belt. "Andy, let's try to injure her wings with our knives. Darko, use your arrows." Andy gave Zoey a nod, and together, they snatched their daggers. Darko readied his bow.

Andy squinted into his shield at the monster's wings. "Just don't hit Spencer."

"Wouldn't dream of it," Zoey said.

They threw the weapons at Medusa, while Darko sent a few arrows her way. They all missed pitifully.

Diana conjured a large sphere of light with her free hand and faced Medusa, keeping her eyes down. "Take this." She threw the light. Medusa darted to the side. The attack blasted the ceiling of the cave, and the walls began to shake.

The cavern cracked and groaned. Dirt, rocks, and glow worms rained on their heads. With a wave of panic, Andy swung around and dashed into the next cavern. "Run!" The ceiling collapsed. Behind him, Medusa laughed, her snakes still hissing.

CHAPTER TEN

ALLY

Zoey's heart raced as she ran from Medusa.

She stumbled over rocks and dips, weaving left and right, the sound of hissing snakes stalking her like a giant cat. Andy and Darko ran ahead of her. Where Spencer and Diana were, she had no idea, nor did she know if they were even still alive. Had they been crushed under the crumbling rocks of the ceiling? Had Medusa turned them to stone? She tried to look back in the reflection of her shield without slowing her pace, but all she could see was glow worms strung across the cave and angel wings as they flapped behind her.

After what seemed like an eternity, she, Andy, and Darko reached a jagged slope in the cave. At the bottom, a new cavern waited, hosting even more of the glow worms. They scrambled down the slope and into the cavern, and as they reached the bottom, they splashed into a pool of freezing, murky water that reached Zoey's hips.

Medusa's hissing grew so loud it echoed off the walls.

Zoey grabbed her axe and threw up her shield, watching the reflection. She held her breath, shivering from the cold water, and caught a quick glance of writhing snakes and a silk dress swooping into the cavern.

Medusa landed in the water and slow-clapped. "I must say, you-ou three have survived far longer than any others who dare give me company. But it is no matter. You will all stay here with me. Forever, with me. Hehe."

Darko glared at her through Andy's shield. His eyes filled with tears. "You killed my brother. It's not fair. He didn't do anything to you, and you killed him."

Medusa threw her head back, letting out something akin to a scream and a cackle. "You know nothing of injustice. I was once a beautiful maiden, wanted by many men. So many, in fact, Poseidon himself took interest in me. He pursued me, and I fled to Athena's temple, begging her to protect me from his advances. But she did not answer my prayer, and Poseidon raped me there. Do you know what Athena did to me then? She transformed me into a monster. And *she's* supposed to be the Goddess of Wisdom. The world is cruel. It's only fair we all suffer, one way or another."

Darko closed his eyes, tears rolling down his cheeks. "Is that why nothing ever seems to go the right way?"

Andy grabbed Darko by the shoulder and looked at him through the shield's reflection. "Don't listen to her, Darko. She's wrong."

Medusa hissed and darted toward Andy, then knocked

his sword from his hands. It splashed into the pool. Darko grabbed an arrow from his bag, closed his eyes, and unleashed a battle cry, blindly lunging for Medusa. She shoved Darko into the pool, then seized Andy by the wrists. She swung him around to face her, but he'd shut his eyes tight.

Zoey clenched her jaw. She could handle her city and everyone in it being destroyed. She could handle finding out that Greek gods were real and that she was the key to a prophecy determining the fate of the world. But she couldn't bear the thought of losing Andy. He'd offered his friendship even though he knew most of the kids in school despised her, and he was the only person she could truly share the burden of saving the world with.

"Look into my eyes!" Medusa screeched in his face.

Zoey spun around and raised her axe, keeping her eyes down. She tried to recall the skills she'd had in Spencer's visions, then mustered all her strength and swung at Medusa's arm once, twice. The satisfying sound of crunching scales filled her ears. Sticky black liquid squirted from Medusa's skin, and the monster screamed in pain. She let go of Andy and clutched her bleeding shoulder, her cries shaking the cavern. Andy took a deep breath, plugged his nose, and jumped into the pool.

New energy surged through Zoey's veins, as if she'd drunk way too much caffeine and needed to do three hours of cardio. She turned and looked into her shield, preparing to chop off the monster's head. But to her dismay, Medusa didn't cower in fear.

The monster leapt into the air. Her wings were extended like those of a bloodthirsty vulture. She flapped toward the ceiling, then dove toward Zoey, her scream a ghoul's in the night. Zoey darted to the side, but Medusa seized her by the wrists with hands as rough as sandpaper and dragged her into the air.

Zoey shut her eyes, wrestling blindly against the monster, every muscle in her body pulled tight. She opened her mouth to scream. Before anything came from her throat, there was a loud *slice*. Medusa cried out and released Zoey. They crashed into the pool.

Water flooded Zoey's nostrils and mouth. Her lungs burned. She broke the surface, Medusa's furious wails ringing in her ears. She opened her eyes and held up her shield, searching for the monster in its reflection, coughing up water and gasping for breath. She caught sight of Medusa, black blood seeping from gaping wounds where her wings had once been. She hissed and splashed toward Andy; her blood covered the sword in his hand. Darko stood behind him, soaking wet. He shot an arrow toward Medusa's head, but she dodged it and advanced.

Zoey twirled around, keeping her eyes down. In one swift movement she rammed the axe into Medusa's neck. There was a *crunch* as the blade went through her scales and bone, separating her head from her body. Zoey snatched the head by a handful of "hair" as it fell, avoiding its gaze, and the little snakes let out a collective scream, then writhed and convulsed before finally going limp. The rest of the body shuddered and collapsed, water splashing around it.

Zoey let out a breath of relief. Andy waded carefully through the water toward her, then pulled off his sweatshirt and offered it. She took it, wrapped Medusa's head with it, and tied the sleeves to make sure it remained secure.

She turned to Darko. His eyes were watery. "I'm sorry," he said, his voice small. "I was no help to you. This was supposed to be my mission, but I couldn't even kill her in the end."

"Don't be silly," Zoey said. "You were so brave. Phoenix would be proud." She held the head out to him. "Take it."

Darko's eyes widened. "Why would you give that to *me*?"

"I want you to keep it safe for us, in case we may need it," Zoey said, smiling.

Andy rested his hand on Darko's shoulder. "You're a part of our group now."

Darko bit his lip. He took the head, then stuffed it into the sack on his back.

Prickling dread creeped through Zoey as she remembered they'd lost the rest of the group. "Crap. We left behind Spencer and Diana. I don't even know— What if they're hurt? We have to go back." As she finished her sentence, golden light as brilliant and hot as the sun flashed in the entrance and filled the cavern. She closed her eyes, stumbling backward.

"Diana?" Andy called.

All around them, the smooth, melodious voice of a man echoed off the walls. "Greetings, Chosen Ones."

"You're not Diana," Darko said.

"No, I am not. But I am your ally nonetheless."

Zoey snorted, peeking through her fingers to see that the light had faded just enough to not burn her eyes, leaving a floating sun the size of a fruit bowl at the entrance of the cavern. Sparks danced around it, like Diana's spheres of light. "If you're really our ally, then why are you hiding from us? Come out," she said, looking around for the man the voice belonged to.

The man chuckled, the sun bobbing up and down as if it were laughing itself. "My body is not manifested here. It can't be, or I would risk being discovered. I am spread thin, only able to send a small amount of power to you in your time of need."

Andy brandished his sword. "What do you want?"

The sun floated up the slope they'd come from. "I want to make certain you find your way back to your demigod friends so you may continue safely on your journey."

The group exchanged shocked glances, scrambling after the sun. "Are they okay?" Zoey cried, her voice wavering. Diana was a fantastic mentor, full of determination, and willing to sacrifice herself for Zoey and Andy. Albeit a little harsh sometimes, she was still great. And Spencer had shared such personal memories with them, memories Zoey was sure he wasn't comfortable rehashing, just so they could learn to fight. The thought of him made her heart skip. Yeah, he hadn't wanted them to go on the mission to slay Medusa, and he could be a real jerk when he was upset, but she still thought he was amazing too.

She hadn't known either of them for very long, but she couldn't imagine what she'd do or how she'd feel if anything were to happen to them. Like Andy, they were important to her.

The sun reached the top of the slope and paused. "Yes, they are alive, but unable to reach you."

Andy furrowed his brow. "Who are you?"

"I cannot say, for fear I will be discovered. If that happens, I will not be able to help any of you again, I'm afraid. Now come, follow me."

They retraced their steps, finally reaching the cavern they'd left Diana and Spencer in. Rocks from the ceiling almost blocked the other side, piled in a heap. Spencer and Diana were sprawled on the ground unconscious. Dirt and sweat covered Spencer, his skin ashen. Blood trickled from a nasty gash on Diana's forehead.

Zoey and Andy cried their names, their voices shaking. Before either of them could race to the demigods' sides, the sun beat them to it. It dumped itself like syrup on the demigods' beaten bodies. Within seconds, its light enveloped them, glowing brighter and brighter. A loud hum vibrated through the cavern, and Zoey's teeth chattered.

Without warning, the hum stopped, and the light died. Zoey glanced around the cavern. The sun was gone.

She stepped toward the demigods. They were still unconscious, but completely unscathed. The sound of her shoes splashing in the pool of the cavern floor echoed off the walls. "Spencer? Diana? Are you guys okay?"

For a moment, her only response was unnerving silence. Then, finally, the demigods' eyes fluttered open. They blinked as if adjusting their vision and looked at Zoey and Andy with wide eyes.

A wave of relief washed over Zoey. She tossed aside her axe and shield, then ran toward them, fighting back tears. She threw her arms around their necks, tackling them in a hug. "I'm so glad you guys are okay."

Diana chuckled weakly, patting Zoey on the back. "Yes, everything's fine." She pulled out of the hug. Spencer gave Zoey a little squeeze, then pulled away as well. Zoey's cheeks grew hot.

"What happened?" Spencer asked. "Where's Medusa?"

Andy patted the sack on Darko's back, and Darko grinned. "Dead," they said in unison. Spencer's and Diana's jaws dropped. Zoey and Andy explained what had happened, and they began their trek out of the cave.

"Let me get this straight," Diana said. "Medusa chased you, you slayed her, and then a talking sun appeared and brought you back to us?"

Zoey dragged her feet. She shivered, not fully dry from the pool of cold water, her muscles already sore. "That's right. It also did this weird thing, like it dumped itself on your bodies. Then it disappeared, and you guys woke up completely uninjured."

Diana bit her lip. "Was the sun— What did its voice sound like?"

Andy brushed his hair back. "Deep. It was definitely a man's voice. But smooth, like calming music."

Spencer shot Diana a serious look. "Your father already helped us once, when you prayed to him. Maybe he's been following us ever since. Maybe he's watching over you. That's the only explanation for how it healed us."

Diana frowned. "Did he mention why he wouldn't show himself?"

"He was spread thin," Darko said from behind. "He couldn't give us his name, for fear he'd be discovered helping us."

For the rest of the trip out of the cave, and for the rest of the evening as they tried to catch up for the time they'd lost, then trained, Diana barely spoke a word. Zoey guessed she was deep in thought, wondering about her father, but didn't press her to talk.

For the next few days, they continued their journey toward Deltama Village. They walked during the day and trained at night, and thanks to more of Spencer's visions, Zoey and Andy were able to spar for almost ten minutes without being knocked down. Even Darko joined in on the fights.

By morning of their seventh day since meeting Persephone, they still hadn't found the tall log gates of the village, and Spencer decided he would try to contact her and ask for a few more days to find it. He gathered a sacrifice for her. They found a small waterfall flowing into a stream, wildflowers growing at its edge, and Diana made a fire next to it. Spencer dropped the berries into the flames.

"Persephone, please come to me," Spencer said. "I need to speak with you." The fire sighed, the flames retreated, and from the smoke Persephone appeared. More wildflowers bloomed at her feet.

She narrowed her eyes at the group. "Why have you summoned me? Why haven't you reached the village yet?"

"We've run into some—*obstacles*," Spencer said. "Could you give us a few more days to reach Hades?"

Persephone pressed her lips into a thin line. "I've already been in Hades for two nights. If I stay here much longer, my mother will surely discover where I've gone and uncover our plan." Her gaze softened, and she took Spencer's hands. "I'm sorry, my child, but I cannot grant your request."

"What happens if we can't find the village in time?" Diana asked. "Or what if they don't let us use their pegasi?"

"Then you will have to fight Hades on your own," Persephone said. "I cannot risk the gods figuring out our plans. I'm sorry." She pulled her hands from Spencer's. "I must go. You have two days. For now I will continue with our plan, but if you don't arrive by the ninth day, your opportunity will be gone." She disappeared.

A *whoosh* sounded above their heads, then the neighing of a horse. The group snapped to attention, trying to spot the creature, but there was only empty sky and a sea of trees.

Darko grinned, his eyes sparkling. "That was a pegasus."

Spencer eyed the trees. "Maybe it can lead us to the village."

"Or maybe we don't have to go to the village at all," Diana said, snapping her fingers. "Pegasi usually travel in groups. If we could track that one, maybe we could capture its friends and then fly to Hades today."

The trees behind them rustled, and Zoey swung around, raising her axe. What was it this time? What new monster was about to terrorize them?

But what stepped out from the trees was no monster. It was a girl.

Zoey guessed she was around twenty years old. She stood nearly as tall as Spencer, thin as a twig, with wavy black hair falling past her hips and round eyes so dark her pupils got lost in the irises. Her skin was a warm medium-brown shade, and she wore a purple crop top and loose pants. A glittering amethyst rested between her thick eyebrows.

The girl shot them a threatening glare, clutching a knife at her side. "What was that about a village? Capturing pegasi?" Her voice was as sharp as the weapon in her hand. "Who do you people think you are?"

CHAPTER ELEVEN

VILLAGE

Andy unsheathed his sword. Since meeting Vanessa, he hadn't seen any new people, but now a girl with long hair and dark eyes had a knife drawn on him and his friends. However, after surviving the Stymphalian Birds and helping slay Medusa, he was confident that if the girl tried to attack them, she'd be defeated easily.

Diana readied her bow. "I don't think you're in any position to be asking the questions here."

The girl rolled her eyes. "If you knew who I was, you'd be on your knees begging for mercy, Princess. What are you doing traveling through the forest like this?"

Diana huffed. "I could ask you the same question. And, by the way, if you knew who *I* was—"

"I'll go first, then. My name is Kali," the girl said, smirking. "I'm the daughter of a chief of a nearby village. My pegasi, Ajax and Aladdin, were out exploring, and I just came to fetch them for dinner." As if on cue, the trees on the other side of the stream rustled. Two pegasi with chestnut coats, black manes and feathered wings, and pretty amber eyes trotted out from them, then leapt over the stream toward Kali. They nickered affectionately at her, and she stroked their necks. "Now tell me, who are you?"

Diana glared at Kali, bow still drawn. "That's none of your business. If you'll excuse us, we were just leaving."

Kali smirked. "None of my business? You're in my territory. Why so secretive, huh, Princess?"

Diana stomped her foot. "How dare you address me as such."

Spencer rested a hand on Diana's shoulder, flashing Kali a quick smile of apology. "You said you come from a nearby village?" She nodded. "My name is Spencer. My group and I are trying to reach a village. May I ask which one you're from?"

"Deltama Village," Kali replied. "There aren't many left around here."

"You have a lot of pegasi in Deltama Village, then?"

Kali narrowed her eyes. "What do you want?"

"We're on a very important mission, one that's a bit time sensitive," Spencer said.

"What kind of important mission?"

"We're going to Hades," he continued. "We have a plan to fight the gods. It's part of a prophecy. And we were looking for some pegasi so we could reach the underworld by the day after tomorrow."

Kali's jaw dropped. "You mean the prophecy that was foretold years ago? You plan to—You're planning a war on the gods?" The group nodded. "Come with me. If what you say is true, perhaps my father will allow you to use our pegasi for your journey."

By late afternoon, the group approached Deltama Village.

The wall around the village was as tall as the trees and miles long, made of logs from the forest. A guy around Kali's age, who was as tall and thin as her, swung down from a watchtower at the front gate and opened it for them to come in.

The whole trip there, Andy hadn't been sure what to expect. Kali was taking them to a legitimate village inhabited by legitimate people that was somewhat thriving in a world destroyed by Greek gods. What was he supposed to expect? Was it modern? Medieval? Were the people friendly, rude, somewhere in between? Hopefully they'd be allowed to borrow a few pegasi. Otherwise, Persephone wouldn't be able to help them and they'd have to fight the King of the Underworld all on their own.

Torches blazed at every corner of the village, a wide variety of people working away, all shapes, sizes, and colors. They wore loose-fitting tops and pants much like Kali's, jewels of all shades between their eyebrows. Their houses were classic log cabins, with gardens full of fruits and vegetables, clothes strung out to dry between them.

Andy shot Zoey a sideways glance. She watched the people in silent awe, her eyes sparkling. He grinned and nudged her shoulder, and she turned to him, flashing a smile that warmed his insides.

The young man who let them in approached the group, eyeing them with suspicion. "Kali, who are these people? Why have you brought them here?"

Kali stroked Aladdin's and Ajax's necks as if they were her pet dogs. "There's no time to explain, Dev. They must speak to my father immediately."

Dev raised an eyebrow, then gestured toward a path down the center of the village. "I'm still on watch duty, so I can't go with you, but he's in his cabin."

They walked down the path for a half hour, winding through crowds, houses, and gardens until they reached more gates guarding a giant four-story cabin. Fiery torches and red-clothed men holding spears stood at the entrance.

Aladdin and Ajax trotted off to play with some giggling village children. Kali smiled, waving at the guards, and they allowed the group to pass through the gates and up to the cabin's door. Kali knocked, and the door creaked open.

The man standing in the entryway was probably the most intimidating guy Andy had seen yet. He was even taller than Spencer and looked like a bodybuilder, with muscles upon muscles bulging from his huge body. His dark hair was dreaded and long, almost longer than Kali's, with bits of silver shining through. The yellow jewel on his wrinkled forehead consumed all the space between his eyebrows, and he wore what looked like a mountain lion's coat around his neck. His irises were so dark they blended in with his pupils, just like Kali's.

"Daughter," he said in a deep voice far less intimidating than his appearance, pulling Kali into a hug. "Who are these people?"

Kali gave him a squeeze. "Let them inside and they'll explain everything. It's very important."

He pulled out of their hug and turned toward the group. "I am Chief Agni, ruler of Deltama Village. Come in. Tell me everything."

The inside of the cabin was cozy, woven rugs with swirling designs and fluffy couches scattered throughout. A fireplace crackled on the back wall, lighting the room.

As they walked inside, five young women stared at them with wide eyes. Chief Agni took a seat on a couch, waving his arm at them. "Run along, ladies. My daughter says these folks have something important to tell me." The girls scattered up the stairs or into other rooms. Chief Agni crossed his arms and turned his gaze to the group. "Why have you come here?"

Spencer bowed. "We're traveling to Hades for an important mission. One that could determine the fate of the world."

Agni raised his eyebrows. "Which is?"

Diana stepped forward. "Spencer and I are demigods guiding the two mortals foretold to lead a war on the gods. We spoke to the Fates a week ago, and they told us that to defeat the gods, the mortals must steal the gods' three main objects of power. The Helm of Darkness, Poseidon's

Trident, and the Lightning Bolt. We're traveling to Hades first to steal the Helm. We only have until the day after tomorrow, and the only way to get there would be on the backs of pegasi, which, as I'm sure you can already tell, we don't have any of."

Agni blinked several times, his jaw opening and closing in shock. "The prophecy? I thought for sure— I thought we wouldn't see it in this lifetime. Who are— Are you . . ." He looked at Andy and Zoey. "Are you two from the Before Time?"

Zoey smirked and linked her arm with Andy's. His heart fluttered at the touch. "Yes," she said. "We came from the year 2018. We died in the Storm, but a demigod daughter of Poseidon sacrificed herself to bring us back to life."

Kali's eyes crinkled with glee, and Agni stood. "This is cause for celebration," he said. "We must prepare a feast for tonight, a feast for the whole village. And tomorrow we'll send you with as many pegasi as you need for the journey ahead." Andy let out a deep breath, relief washing over him.

The group exchanged excited glances, and Spencer bowed again. "Thank you so much, Chief Agni. You will be remembered as a great hero amongst all who oppose the gods."

Chief Agni smiled. "You're more than welcome. Anything to bring down those wretched demons." He called down a few servant girls, then turned to Kali. "Get them cleaned up. I'll have the guards instruct our villagers to prepare for the celebration."

Kali ushered Zoey and Diana away, while some servant girls led Andy, Spencer, and Darko up the stairs into a plain washroom with three bathtubs and a few mirrors lit by candles. The servants soon fetched them hot water, soap, towels, and fresh sets of clothes.

The young men quickly bathed, and Andy made a point to scrape his body of the nasty muck he'd acquired from the journey. Soon they were clean, and they dressed themselves, their outfits loose and orange.

Darko's stomach growled. He clutched it and grimaced. "Hopefully we'll eat soon. I'm starving."

"I'm sure we will," Spencer said, standing near the door. "Chief Agni mentioned a feast."

Andy sighed. Every muscle in his body ached. "Yeah, I'm just glad we finally made it to the village, and that we get to borrow some pegasi. Just thinking about walking makes my legs feel like noodles."

Darko bit his fingernails. "So am I going with you to Hades? Or do I have to stay here?"

Andy shot Spencer a glance, then crossed his arms and looked to the floor. "I don't even know if we'll survive the trip. I'm not sure it's safe for you to go."

Darko dropped his hands to his sides and slumped his shoulders. "Oh, okay."

Someone knocked on the door, and a few giggling servant girls poked their heads into the room. "The celebration will begin shortly," one chirped. "Chief Agni wants you downstairs as soon as possible."

"Andy and I will be down in a moment," Spencer said. "You can go, Darko." Andy raised his eyebrows, confused, and Darko nodded, then followed the servants out of the washroom and shut the door behind him.

Spencer turned to Andy. "Before we go down there, I just wanted to say how proud I am of you and Zoey." He rested a hand on Andy's shoulder. "You've come a long way since I met you. I mean . . . you went from almost getting yourself killed by the Amphisbaena to helping slay *Medusa*, of all monsters, without my and Diana's help. I guess what I'm trying to say is I look forward to continuing your training and watching you grow."

Andy blinked in surprise. He wasn't sure what he'd expected Spencer to say, but he didn't think it would be so kind, especially since Andy hadn't acted the nicest during their argument a few days ago.

"Uh, thank you," Andy said. "I look forward to that too." And he meant it, no matter how irritated he got over the way Zoey treated Spencer, or how many more times they would disagree over something.

Spencer gave him a warm, genuine smile. Suddenly he didn't seem like a gloomy Son of Hades; he seemed more like a regular guy Andy and Mark would have played video games with on a Saturday night. "Let's head downstairs and go to this party. We deserve to relax at least a little bit before we go to Hades."

* ~ * ~ * ~

Kali dragged Zoey and Diana all the way to the fourth level of the cabin, then shoved them into a washroom lit by several candles, complete with two tubs and a mirror.

Despite the room's rustic appearance, Zoey was grateful she'd be allowed to bathe at all, eager to scrape every last bit of dirt and sweat from her tired body.

"Wait here," Kali said, grinning. "Our servants will bring you some soap and hot water to fill your baths shortly. I'll try to find you some clean clothes for the celebration." She looked Diana up and down. "Although I don't think anyone in the village is near as tiny as you, Princess."

Diana huffed and crossed her arms. "I already told you, my name is Diana, Daughter of Apollo. And I'll be fine in what I'm wearing, thank you very much."

Kali chuckled. "You haven't had a change of clothes in days, let alone a bath. Trust me, I'll find you something. You'll smell better." Diana's jaw dropped, her eyes flaring with anger. Kali winked, scampered out of the washroom, and closed the door behind her. Diana pouted like a bratty toddler.

Zoey burst out laughing. "She has a point. We probably smell disgusting." She looked in the mirror, catching a glance of her unkept curls lumping together with dust. Her jeans and flannel had tons of tears in them and were covered with grime. "We certainly aren't looking our best."

Diana balled her fists, her cheeks turning firetruck

red. "That *girl* is absolutely infuriating. If it weren't for the fact that we need their pegasi, I'd have already blasted her across the forest." Zoey giggled. She had a feeling that wasn't what Diana really thought about Kali.

The door burst open, and eight young women with buckets of water, dry rags, towels, and bars of sweet-smelling soap rushed into the room. They dumped the water into the tubs, then set everything else on the floor. They turned to Zoey and Diana and bowed. "Let us know if there's anything else you require," one said. "Kali will be back soon with your change of clothes." They scurried out of the washroom.

Zoey and Diana bathed, and once they were done, they sat on the floor wrapped in their towels, waiting for Kali to bring their change of clothes.

Zoey smiled, finally squeaky clean. "What do you think the celebration will entail?"

Diana tucked her hair behind her ears. "Food. Talking. Music. Dancing. The typical stuff." She paused and turned to Zoey, smirking. "Hey, if there is dancing, you should dance with Andy."

"What do you mean? Like, as friends?"

Diana shoved her. "No. As a couple."

Zoey wrinkled her nose, disgusted at the thought. Not that Andy was disgusting, he was cute, but she didn't like him that way. She hated to admit it, but if she was interested in anyone, it was Spencer. She'd tried to avoid guys at all costs since dating Jet—not that she'd had time for guys, anyway—but she felt herself more drawn to Spencer with each passing day.

She slumped her shoulders. It was never going to happen, obviously. The love of his life had died only a short while ago, and for a crazy good cause. He'd probably never get over her, and she didn't expect him to. She couldn't force something like that; it would be cruel and selfish.

Besides, she had more important things to worry about than crushes. Like getting to Hades, stealing the Helm of Darkness, and taking Darko to Alikan Village.

"No way," Zoey said. "I don't think of Andy like that. He's my friend."

Diana laughed. "Oh dear. Well, he doesn't think of you as just a friend. He's pretty much in love with you, and I think he has been for a long time."

Zoey's stomach dropped. "What? How do you know that?"

"Anyone with sense can tell. Do you have any sense?"

Zoey rolled her eyes and elbowed Diana in the arm. "Shut up."

For a few minutes they sat in silence, before finally, Zoey let out a sad sigh.

"What's wrong?" Diana asked.

Zoey shook her head, thinking about what Andy said when they'd first met. How he didn't believe any of the "rumors" surrounding her. She wondered if he would still want to be her friend if he knew they were true, even if he knew why she did what she did. "It's nothing."

Diana turned to Zoey and narrowed her eyes. "No. Something's wrong. What is it?"

Zoey frowned, her gaze drifting to the floor. Could she talk to Diana about what she'd done? Would Diana still like her? Would she still think Zoey was worthy of fighting the gods? Of saving the world? Or would she throw Zoey aside? Would she turn up her nose and torment her forever, just like everyone at school? Just like her own mother?

Zoey didn't want to take that chance, but had a feeling she'd be pressured to confess what happened. She opened her mouth, ready to tell Diana everything from start to finish, but then the door creaked open.

They looked up, and there stood Kali, a bundle of clothes in her arms. "I found something small enough to fit Diana."

* ~ * ~ * ~

When Andy and Spencer met with Darko and the chief downstairs, Zoey, Diana, and Kali were nowhere to be seen. Andy wanted to ask where they were, but the chief brought them out to the other side of the cabin. The sun had set and the moon glowed in the night. A group of guards swarmed them.

The guards led them through the village down more winding paths, in the opposite direction from which they came, the residents buzzing with excitement as they prepared for what Andy assumed was part of the celebration.

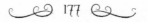

Men hung strings of lights between the roofs of cabins, while children set out clay lamps carved with delicate swirls on porches. Groups of women huddled together in the gardens, whispering to each other as they balanced pots on their heads and picked fruits and vegetables. Above all the commotion, pegasi neighed, and Andy looked up to see around ten of them, all different colors, flapping their wings as they flew through the sky.

Andy smiled, awed by the village's beauty. It was the most cheerful thing he'd seen since waking up from the Storm. The people were normal, happy, talkative. No one was screaming, crying, or dead. No one seemed to be scared of being turned to stone or eaten by a giant bird, and Andy finally felt at ease. At least, as much as he could be. They still had a lot to do before their quest was over, and he still had to get his family back.

They reached a wide, circular clearing void of cabins, lined with blazing torches and strings of lights and pretty clay lamps. Men and women worked there, too, setting up drums, tuning string instruments, and stirring food in pots hung over a fire. The guards stopped. A few went to help set things up, while the rest lingered around Chief Agni.

Andy cleared his throat, about to ask where Zoey and Diana were, but then someone tapped him on the shoulder. He whipped around in surprise, and for a moment he forgot to breathe.

Zoey stood before him, a dazzling smile on her lips, her curly brown hair to the side in a neat braid. Her loose teal crop top and pants hugged her pronounced curves in all the right ways and made her tan skin glow. Her sky-blue eyes sparkled brighter than he'd ever seen.

She squealed. "Can you believe how gorgeous the lights are, Andy? Kali said there might be fireworks."

Diana stepped up beside Zoey. She frowned, her arms crossed. Her hair was also braided to the side, and she wore a blush-pink dress that reached her mid-thigh. "Yippee."

Andy broke from his trance and laughed at Diana. "What's your problem?"

Kali appeared next to him, a mischievous grin on her lips. "Oh, Princess here is upset we confiscated her clothes."

Diana shot Kali a piercing glare. "How am I supposed to fight monsters in this?"

Spencer sighed and rubbed his temples. "You've worn a dress before. I think you'll be okay."

She stomped her foot. "It's not the fact that it's a dress. It's the fact that it's pink."

Kali put her hands on her hips, still smiling. "Well, don't worry. Our servants will have your regular clothes ready for you in the morning. But they need a good wash and some patching up first."

Men, women, children, and even a few pegasi began to fill the clearing. Many of them carried yummy-smelling treats, pots of steaming soup, bowls and plates, and eating utensils. Guards jumped to attention and filed in toward Chief Agni, Kali, and the group, then stood around them in a protective formation.

Once the clearing was full and the villagers had, for the most part, settled down, Chief Agni pushed himself through his guards and held out his arms. "My people," he said, his voice carrying a long way. Everyone quieted and looked to him. "Tonight, we celebrate the arrival of two mortals brought forward in time, foretold to lead a war on the Greek gods." He paused, but not for dramatic effect. The villagers cheered and clapped.

After they quieted again, he continued, "I believe if they are able to succeed in their plans, they stand a chance against those unholy demons. And when the world finally belongs to humanity, perhaps we may live in peace, knowing not a single monster will come for us again. Now, let's enjoy the night." He pumped his fists in the air, and the villagers cheered, this time even louder. Andy covered his ears. It was like a football stadium during the Super Bowl.

After a few minutes of cheering, the village erupted with music. The men and women who'd set up the drums and stringed instruments played away. Some people danced, some filled plates with food and handed them out, and some talked and laughed amongst each other.

* ~ * ~ * ~

For the next few hours, Zoey talked with villagers, laughed until her sides hurt, and ate until she could hardly walk.

Eventually she decided to stand alone on the sidelines and watch people as they enjoyed themselves. Spencer and Andy had been dragged away by some guys who wanted to talk, and Darko had pulled Diana into the crowd to dance with him. It was no problem; she planned to find them again later.

She spotted Kali shaking her hips and twisting her arms in a seductive belly dance with the young man named Dev around one of the fires, and smiled.

Kali noticed Zoey, then stopped dancing and rushed toward her. "What are you doing all by yourself?" she yelled over the crowd.

Zoey shifted her weight. "Just trying to let this food go through me. It's been a while since I've eaten that much. Well, it's been a while since I've had good food, period. Diana's idea of a good dinner is burnt rabbit. Every. Single. Night. I mean, there's the occasional squirrel, but still."

Kali shook her head, a twinkle in her eye. "That girl is something else."

Zoey smirked. "You have no idea. So, I need to know, how has this village survived so long? How are you guys doing so well? Everyone else seems to be struggling big-time. I mean, I guess if they weren't, we wouldn't need to fight the gods. What are you guys doing that works?"

Kali shrugged. "We live really close to Hades. Most villages don't because they're afraid, so it's pretty rare for monsters to pass through."

"And Hades—the god—has never come out and attacked you?"

"I'm not sure he knows we exist, but he can't leave the underworld unless Zeus permits it."

"You said it's rare for monsters to pass through. How often does that happen, then?"

Kali's expression darkened, and her gaze drifted to the ground. "Maybe once every ten to fifteen years. The last time it happened was three years ago. I was seventeen years old. It was Lamia . . ."

"Lamia? What's that?"

"A woman who, in the old days, was unfairly punished by Zeus's wife, Hera. She was his mistress, and Hera killed all her children and turned her into a child-eating monster. Somehow she found us, and she snuck up on a few of our kids while they were fetching water from the stream outside the gates. They were taking so long, and when we found them . . . their bodies . . ." Her eyes filled with tears. "I can't even describe to you how awful it was. After that, a few of my father's soldiers and I hunted her down. It took weeks, but when I found her, I showed no mercy."

Zoey shook her head. "That's awful."

Kali nodded. "Children aren't allowed outside the gates without a guard now."

"And—your pegasi—how did you guys get so many?"

Kali's face lit up. "We traded for a few a long time ago and have bred them ever since."

Someone tapped Zoey's shoulder. She spun around to find Andy there, smiling. She couldn't be sure, but it seemed as if he was being flirtatious, his cheeks flushed. "Hey," he said.

Her heart fluttered. Had he always looked at her like that, or was she just now noticing because of what Diana told her? "Uh. Hi."

He held out his hand to her and jerked his head toward the hordes of twirling people. "Wanna dance with me?"

Zoey's cheeks grew hot, and she shrank back. "Oh, uh— I don't know . . . I'm not the best dancer."

Andy rolled his eyes. "Neither am I, but that doesn't mean we can't have a good time." He seized her hands and pulled her into the crowd of dancing villagers. Before she could process what had happened, dozens of bodies surrounded her, and Andy twirled her around as if she were weightless. For a while they danced, their bodies close, their hands intertwined.

Zoey tripped over her feet and stumbled to the side. Andy caught her by the waist. He pulled her up, their faces so close she could feel his breath on her cheek.

"Got ya," he said, blushing.

Her breath caught in her throat. "Thanks." He pulled her chest against his, his stormy gray eyes locked on her.

Someone tapped her on the shoulder. She turned, and her heart leapt in her chest.

It was Spencer.

He cleared his throat. "Hey, Zoey. Could I talk to you? Privately?"

She pulled away from Andy, her stomach twisting.

What did Spencer want to talk to her about? "Yeah, of course." She turned to Andy. His gaze darted between her and Spencer. "Thanks for the dance, Andy. It was a lot of fun. I'll see you later?"

Andy pressed his lips into a thin line. "Yeah, of course."

She swung around, eager to talk with Spencer. He took her by the arm and led her through the crowd.

Soon they reached a somewhat quiet spot void of people and took a seat on a bench in a garden between two cabins. Spencer pulled his arm away, then folded his hands in his lap. Strings of lights twinkled above their heads.

Zoey sucked in a deep breath. "So, what did you need to talk to me about?"

"Remember the night I couldn't talk about Syrena, so I left? Remember how you came and found me, and you asked if I could show you how your father died?"

A lump formed in her throat. "Of course I remember. Why?"

He turned to her, his dark eyes solemn. "I didn't want to show you, because I didn't want to distract you from our mission. I didn't want it to hurt you. I planned to show you once all of this was over. But I'm scared . . ."

She inched closer to him. "What are you scared of?"

"I'm scared I won't be able to."

"Why wouldn't you be able to?"

He shook his head. "It doesn't matter. Do you want to see how he died, or not?"

A million questions swarmed in Zoey's head, but she

knew this might be her only chance to find out what happened to her father. So instead of speaking, she nodded, and Spencer placed his thumb on her forehead. Fog consumed her.

* ~ * ~ * ~

Andy clenched his fists in frustration, standing on the sidelines of the celebration.

Why had Zoey gone off with Spencer? He thought they'd been having a great time dancing. And why did Spencer even ask to talk to her "privately" in the first place? Syrena had died less than two weeks before—how could he just move on like that?

Diana and Darko approached Andy, arm in arm and all smiles. "What are you doing all the way over here?" Diana asked. "I thought you were enjoying yourself."

Andy gritted his teeth. "I was. Zoey and I were dancing, and then Spencer just came up out of nowhere and asked if he could talk to her alone. I knew she had a thing for him, but I had no idea— I mean, I figured he wasn't over Syrena . . ."

Diana rested a hand on Andy's shoulder. "Hey, he's *not* over Syrena. He loves her with everything he has. He probably will until the end of time, and I mean that in the literal sense. I doubt he wanted to whisk Zoey to a romantic getaway. I'm sure it's something else."

Andy relaxed his muscles. "Okay, you're probably

right, then."

Darko grinned. "Kali said they'd be shooting off fireworks in a few minutes. Will you watch them with us?"

Andy forced a smile. "That sounds great."

* ~ * ~ * ~

Zoey barreled through empty black space, voices echoing through the abyss. Familiar voices. The voices of her mother and father.

Her father's voice was just as she remembered. Calm, smooth, as if his vocal cords were smothered in sweet honey, even when he said something unkind. "You're an unfit mother, Tami, and you won't have Zoey for long. Not after I prove to the court you're psychotic."

"I am not psychotic, you insensitive, piece-of-shit bastard!" Tami screeched.

Zoey jolted forward, suddenly inside of a car, sitting in the front passenger seat. She gasped, recognizing it immediately as her father's old silver Taurus. The one he'd taken her to school in every day while singing along with classic rock and eating Pop-Tarts. Those drives were some of her fondest memories, up until she never saw him again. After that, she'd buried them away.

She looked out the windshield and saw it was dark outside, the only light being the car's headlights. The car was on a road through a cornfield, surely in Nebraska, and rain poured from the sky. She gulped, looking at the driver.

It was her dad.

He looked exactly as she remembered. A handsome man with shiny black hair, deep-olive skin, and eyes as blue as a clear midday sky. He held his phone with one hand and steered with the other, talking to her mother. "I'll be willing to allow you visitation rights, but not if you continue to use her against me like this. You're insane, you hear me? Insane, and I won't have you ruining her life like you did mine."

Zoey clutched her chest, heart pounding. He'd wanted her? He'd tried to fight for her? He'd tried to protect her from her mother?

He screamed and spun the steering wheel. His phone tumbled to the floor. The car rolled several times at high speed. Zoey flew through her door and into the rain, then began her ascent toward the sky.

She clawed the air. "Dad!" But the Taurus was turned over in the cornfield. Tears rolled down her cheeks. "*Dad!*"

Fog crept into the corners of her vision and swallowed her whole.

Zoey opened her eyes, the night radiant with colorful fireworks.

Earlier she'd hoped to enjoy them with her comrades, but now that Spencer had shown her what happened to her father, she wanted to do nothing but pound her fists into a punching bag and scream. Her stomach churned, her knuckles white as she gripped the bench beneath her.

Spencer pulled his thumb from her forehead, sweat

rolling down his face. He trembled, staring at her for a moment, his breaths heavy. She stared back, her mouth agape.

She blinked a few times. Her vision grew blurry, her eyes filling with tears. "My dad—he didn't abandon me." Her voice cracked. "He was on his way to get me back from my mom. It was raining, and the car . . . He wrecked our car . . ."

She burst into a fit of sobs, her body shaking in anguish. All those years she'd hated her father, pushing every memory of him out of her mind, practically pretending he didn't exist. On top of that, she didn't only blame her mother for her bad decisions. She blamed him too.

But in that moment, she finally understood none of it was his fault. He'd wanted her; he'd planned to fight for her. And if he'd survived the crash, or if her mother had at least told her what really happened to him, maybe she wouldn't have been so miserable and determined to start her life over all those years, even if she'd still made some bad decisions.

She turned away from Spencer. She'd always been embarrassed to cry in front of people. In fact, she avoided crying in general. But he did something she never expected him to do. He wrapped her in his arms and rested her head against his chest. She buried her face in his silky shirt. Tears streamed down her face, her father's last words lingering in her mind.

They sat together for what seemed like hours, fireworks blasting high above them, wrapped in each other's arms and saying nothing. Eventually Zoey's tears subsided, and she pulled out of their embrace. "Thank you so much. You have no idea what that meant to me."

Spencer smiled. "You're welcome. After everything that's happened, I mean . . . I just didn't want you to lose the chance to know the truth."

She wiped her eyes. "What do you mean by that? Why would I lose the chance?"

"The future isn't predictable. We all plan to get out of Hades alive, but what if you die? What if I die?"

"You're not going to die." She stood. "And neither am I. We've lived through a Stymphalian Birds attack and slayed Medusa. If we have to fight Hades, we'll take him down easily."

Spencer shook his head. "He's an immortal god. You can't go in thinking like that. It's a surefire way to get killed."

Zoey wanted to argue, but before she could say a word, a familiar voice that sent chills down her spine came from behind. "So, Spencer, is that where you're going? To Hades?" She turned around to find none other than Karter, the Son of Zeus, hidden behind them in the shadows.

Spencer jumped to his feet. "Karter? But I thought—I thought I . . ."

Karter stepped into the light, his gold eyes flashing. "Killed me?"

Zoey shook her head in disbelief. "How did you find us? Why are you still following us?"

Karter shot her a glare. "It's of no concern to you, mortal girl." He looked to Spencer. "Please, come to your senses. Stop this while you still have the chance."

"Enough with that already," Spencer said. "I'm never going to serve the gods again, so forget about it and leave us alone."

"You'll be killed," Karter said. "Just like Syrena."

"And you won't be there to stick up for me, like I was for her," Spencer replied. "I know you cared about her, and I know you cared for me too. But you obviously don't care enough about either of us to stand up to the gods, at least anymore."

Karter shook as though a snowstorm raged through his body. He lifted a hand and brushed his scar, then dropped it and balled his fists at his sides. "Fine," he said, his tone so menacing it made Zoey shiver. "If you won't listen to reason . . ." He locked eyes with her. "I'll have to find another way to convince you."

Karter dashed toward Zoey. She darted to the side, but he snatched her around the waist. Spencer grabbed his arm, and she tried to shove Karter off, but he tightened his grip on her and kicked Spencer away.

"Let me go!" she shrieked, thrashing against him. She wished she'd brought her axe and dagger to the party, but she'd left them back in Chief Agni's cabin.

He sneered and hoisted her over his shoulder, then sailed into the chilly night sky.

CHAPTER TWELVE

NIGHTMARE

Andy wanted to enjoy the fireworks with Darko and Diana, but as they flashed through the sky, and as the crowd cheered and clapped, he couldn't help but glance back to where Spencer and Zoey walked off earlier that night. What was taking them so long?

As if on cue, Spencer raced into the clearing, scanning the crowd, his brow furrowed as if in worry. Andy leapt to his feet and wove through the villagers to reach him.

Spencer spotted Andy as he approached. "Where's Kali? Chief Agni? We need some pegasi, now."

"What? Why? Where's Zoey?"

Spencer put his head in his hands. "Karter followed us here, and when I said I wouldn't go back to serving the gods, he grabbed Zoey and flew into the sky before I could stop him."

Andy's stomach dropped. "Wait, what?"

"We have to go after him," Spencer said, then dashed into the crowd. "Kali! Chief Agni!"

Andy and Spencer pushed through the villagers, calling for them. Within a few minutes they showed up, parting the crowd, Diana and Darko trailing behind them. "What is the meaning of this?" Chief Agni boomed. "Why are you two causing such a disturbance?"

"A demigod Son of Zeus kidnapped Zoey," Spencer said. "And before I could grab her from him, he flew into the sky."

Chief Agni's jaw dropped and Kali whistled over the crowd. "I need Ajax and Aladdin," she said. "The girl from the Before Time was kidnapped." The villagers erupted in panicked whispers and scrambled to bring them the pegasi, while Diana and Darko joined Andy and Spencer.

Darko looked up at them. "Will Zoey be all right?" Andy frowned and turned away, unable to answer. If she wasn't all right, that scar-faced freak had no idea what kind of hell Andy planned to unleash.

Diana rested a hand on Andy's shoulder. "Hey, it's going to be okay," she said. "We'll get her back, and we'll take care of Karter."

Andy's nostrils flared. "You're right; we will take care of Karter. I'll rip him to shreds if he does anything to hurt her." Zoey was the reason he'd agreed to go on this insane quest in the first place. Of course, later on he'd decided he really wanted to go so he could save his family, and he'd even decided he wanted to help people in need, people like Vanessa and Darko, but he had no idea how he could press on if something bad happened to her. She hadn't even known his name and she'd stood up for him against Jet. Now she was becoming one of his closest friends, and he hoped one day she'd become more.

Diana's gaze softened. She patted Andy on the back. "Zoey will be okay. I'm sure of it."

"Do you want me to get the head for you so you can turn him to stone?" Darko asked.

Andy nodded, but Spencer shook his head. "No, no. There's not enough time, and I'm sure we can handle Karter on our own. He hasn't tried to hurt anyone yet."

Andy opened his mouth to argue, before several villagers rushed toward them, Kali and Chief Agni close behind. They guided Ajax and Aladdin by the reins, the pegasi's wings folded against their sides. He supposed the sooner they could get to Zoey, the better. "Are any of you experienced in riding pegasi?" Kali asked.

"Spencer and me," Diana said, and pulled away from Andy.

Kali nodded. "Good. You two will be in control, then. Are you all armed?"

Spencer pulled a dagger from his robes, and Andy gestured toward his belt, which held both his sword and knife. Diana shrugged. "No," she said. "I left all my weapons back at the cabin. But my powers are good for combat, so I'll be fine."

Kali took the pegasi's reins and guided them to the group. "Then you must go now. You have to hurry."

Spencer mounted Ajax while Diana hopped onto

Aladdin.

"Please, don't let them get hurt," Kali said.

"We'll do everything we can to keep them safe," Diana replied.

Andy went to climb onto Ajax's back, but stopped when he saw the sad expression on Darko's face as he stood on the sidelines. His lip quivered. "Will you be back soon, Andy?"

Andy stepped toward him and put his hands on Darko's shoulders. "Yes, of course. And once we are, we'll take you to your village. I promise you." And with that, he turned away to climb onto Ajax, determined to save Zoey.

They flew into the black sky, the moon and stars their only light source. Cold air pummeled Andy in the face, his hair whipping backward in the wind. He squinted into the night and searched for any sign of Zoey and Karter.

Within a few minutes he spotted two black figures in the distance as they struggled against each other.

"Is that them?" Diana yelled over the wind.

Spencer squeezed Ajax's sides with his heels, and the pegasus sped up. "I think so."

They caught up to the figures, and Andy could see they were in fact Zoey and Karter. The scar-faced demigod had her thrown over his shoulder, and she pounded her fists against his back, snarling at him to let her go.

When she caught a glimpse of the group, she stopped hitting Karter, rested her arms on his back, and smirked. "You're about to be in a world of hurt."

Karter paused and turned around. His eyes widened when he saw the group flying straight for him. "How did you—how did you get more pegasi?"

Spencer whipped out his dagger, holding tight to Ajax with his other hand. "Let her go!"

Karter curled his lip in a sneer and flew high above them. "Stop this foolishness and align yourself with the gods. Then perhaps I'll consider."

"I'd hoped you'd listen to reason, but it looks like I'll just have to kill you again," Spencer said. Andy drew his knife, and Diana raised a hand and conjured a blazing sphere of light. Together they veered upward.

Diana launched the light straight for Karter's head, but he dodged the attack and jolted through the air. Zoey shrieked. Ajax darted toward Karter, and Andy raised his weapon, anger boiling in his gut. He sliced the air between Karter's legs.

Karter soared backward, then toward the clouds. "You'll have to be quicker than that," he said. Zoey screamed.

Andy snarled, and Spencer kicked Ajax's sides. "Go, after them." Both Ajax and Aladdin neighed, and the group sped toward Karter.

Diana threw another sphere of light, but Karter darted out of the way and laughed. "Nice try, but I've been dodging lightning bolts in training since I was a kid."

Diana conjured another attack, glaring at Karter. "Your face says differently."

A look of pure hate consumed Karter's features. He raised a hand, and lightning danced along his fingertips. "Good one." A gold bolt solidified in his hand. He threw it at Diana. She swerved to the side, but the bolt grazed her shoulder, rocking her body with crackling electricity. She nearly fell off Aladdin, but the pegasus caught her with his wing and struggled through the air to keep from falling. She lay unconscious, smoke curling off her body.

Blood pounded in Andy's ears. Would Diana be okay? She'd done so much to help them, to teach them. He couldn't imagine losing her, even if he hadn't known her for very long. "No!" he cried. Zoey thrashed her arms and kicked her legs. Karter's jaw fell, and he stared at his hand as if in shock.

"I'll send you to Hades for that," Spencer said through clenched teeth. Ajax bolted straight for Karter. Andy and Spencer raised their knives and jabbed at Karter's legs, but the demigod dodged them, dropping several feet. Ajax spun around and fell to Karter's level. Andy sliced the air again, and as they crossed paths he stabbed Karter in the thigh. Karter screamed and dropped another hundred feet. Zoey looked up at Andy and Spencer with fear in her eyes, reaching for them.

Spencer put away his dagger and kicked Ajax's sides. "Down, Ajax!" The pegasus dove for Karter and Zoey. Spencer extended his hand toward her. Just as their fingers brushed, Karter regained his composure and yanked her out of Spencer's grasp. Andy snarled and swung the blade of his dagger against the demigod's side. Karter screamed again, blood spurting from his wounds. Zoey wriggled from his grasp and leapt into Spencer's outstretched arms. Ajax neighed and fell a few feet, his breaths growing heavy.

Karter clutched his wound, his head bobbing as though he struggled to stay conscious. Spencer stroked Ajax's mane. "C'mon, buddy. Stay strong. We're almost done." He squeezed his heels against Ajax's sides. "Good-bye, Karter."

Ajax neighed and bolted toward Karter. He raised his hooves, then kicked the demigod backward. Karter fell, limbs flailing, into the forest below.

Andy reached over Spencer's shoulder and took Zoey's hand. "Are you okay?"

She trembled. "Yeah, I'm fine. But Diana . . ."

They all looked up at Aladdin and Diana. He'd managed to get her on his back, and he descended toward the forest floor, careful to keep her from falling. They followed.

Once they reached the ground, Spencer leapt off Ajax and plucked Diana from Aladdin's back, his eyes glistening with tears. Where the lightning had struck her shoulder, she was blue and purple, with marks like the twisted branches of a tree extending toward her chest and up her neck. She was even more pale than usual, her breaths shallow and labored.

Andy and Zoey climbed off Ajax. "Is she going to be okay?" Andy asked, his voice cracking. "Can she heal herself?"

Zoey took Diana's hands. "Diana? Please, please, wake up."

The branches above their heads rustled. A raven bolted from them, squawking. It exploded with golden light so blinding Andy had to shield his eyes.

"Greetings, Chosen Ones," sang the deep, melodious voice he recognized as the sun who'd come to them in Medusa's cave. The light faded, and he let his hand drop, opening his eyes. Before them stood a man who looked no older than twenty-five.

He was handsome and ridiculously tall, almost seven feet. His skin was sun kissed, accentuated by the crisp white of his robes, his strawberry-blond hair thick and curly. Rays of gold shone off his toned body as if he were the human embodiment of light itself, and once Andy saw his bright green eyes, he knew exactly who the man was.

Diana's father.

Spencer looked up at him with wide eyes. "Apollo . . ." Apollo took Diana from Spencer's arms.

"Wait, what are you going to do with her?" Andy said. "We need her."

Apollo brushed her hair back. "Not in this state, you don't." The words rolled off his tongue like poetry. "After this horrible a blow, she wouldn't have been able to guide you on your quest. Thankfully, I've been watching over all of you."

"Would the lightning have killed her?" Zoey asked.

Apollo rested Diana on the ground and placed his

hand on her injured shoulder. "The only way Karter could have killed her instantly was if he'd struck her with green lightning, but only a few children of Zeus have ever been powerful enough to create or control green bolts, and he's not one of them."

"But people die from lightning strikes all the time," Andy said. "And I've never heard of their colors mattering at all."

"Lightning created by hand is different from lightning created by Zeus's Master Lightning Bolt," Apollo said. "And the strength of handmade bolts is measured in color. Red is weakest, barely able to burn. Used mostly as a threat. Gold is average, harming the opponent without directly killing them. And green is strongest. Even the slightest touch of a green bolt kills. But Zeus's Master Lightning Bolt is all-powerful. Whoever wields it holds authority over the world. Even the weakest blast from it could kill a mortal. But lightning made by hand . . . It cannot kill unless it is green. It does not come from the heavens."

"That's right," Spencer said. "But getting hit with gold lightning is still pretty bad. Without the proper care, it could get infected. If you hadn't shown up . . ."

Apollo's hand glowed, and Diana's body lit up. "All these years, I've fought alongside the gods, hungry for the ancient power I once possessed. I helped with the Storm, sending golden arrows down from the sky to kill at random." He pulled his hand from Diana. The light coming off her faded, her injuries evaporating. "But after falling in love with Opal, after I wasn't able to save her and she died giving birth to our daughter . . ." His eyes filled with tears. "After feeling that kind of pain, I know I can't lose Diana, whether she's betrayed the gods or not. Which is why, ever since she asked me for help, I've been watching her from afar, protecting her, giving her strength."

"You've been helping us," Zoey said.

Apollo pulled Diana into his arms and held her head against his shoulder. "Yes. I have certainly betrayed the gods, much like my daughter," he said. "And now that I've fully manifested here, they may find out what I've done. If they do, I will be punished severely. Perhaps they'll even put me in Tartarus."

"Tartarus?" Zoey asked. "What's that?"

Spencer turned to her. "It's the deepest section of the underworld, a miserable abyss used like a prison for those who did unthinkable things against the gods, including the Titans."

"Titans?"

Apollo set Diana down. "That's a long story, for another day. And we have no time to waste. You four need to hurry and get to Hades to steal the Helm, before anyone discovers where I am and uncovers your plan. For now, as far as they know, Karter and Spencer are hunting Diana and will have her back to New Mount Olympus for her execution in a few weeks." He snapped his fingers, and light crackled at their feet. The weapons and clothes that they'd left at the village—now clean and riddled with colorful patches—appeared before them.

Zoey grabbed her things. "Thank you so much."

Apollo smiled. "You're welcome. I did not deliver Medusa's head to you for this journey. It will not work on any of the creatures in Hades, even the monsters, as they are all immortal, like the gods themselves. Diana should be awake soon, and once she is, you must go there immediately."

Andy frowned. "Wait, what about the villagers? How will they know we saved Zoey, that we're okay and going to Hades?"

"I will leave them a message for you," Apollo said.

Andy knit his brow, thinking of Darko. "If by some chance we don't make it out of there, will you take Darko to Alikan Village? He's the satyr we slayed Medusa for. I promised we'd take him . . ."

Apollo's eyes grew sad and he opened his mouth to speak, but before he could say anything, Diana's eyes fluttered open. She saw him and shot up. "Dad? What's going on?"

Apollo took her hands. "I've been watching over you ever since you prayed to me. I gave you the power to save your friends from the Stymphalian Birds, I healed you and made sure they reached you in Medusa's cave, and now I've healed you from the lightning bolt you were struck with."

Diana squeezed his hands. "You've risked everything you have, everything you've worked to gain, just to save me? All this time, I thought you hated me for what I did."

Apollo smiled. "Of course not, beloved daughter.

I could never hate you. I wanted you to come home, to forget all of history, to forget the mistakes the gods have made. I did my best to let you grow up happy, ignorant to politics." He sighed and dropped his head. "But I knew nothing would bring you home. You're far too stubborn to change your mind after making such a drastic decision. I had to make a choice. I could either stand by and allow you to get hurt or even die, or I could help you when you most needed me."

Diana wrinkled her nose. "So you thought I couldn't do it on my own?"

Apollo shook his head. "No, my dear. Not at all. But you must understand, after losing your mother . . ." Diana bit her lip and threw her arms around his neck. He closed his eyes, pulling her into a warm embrace. Literally. Within seconds of their hug, light flew off Apollo's glowing body like crackling sparklers.

Diana's eyes grew watery, her voice shaking. "What will Zeus do to you if he finds out you've helped me?"

Apollo pulled out of their hug and rested his hands on her shoulders. The sparks flying off his body faded away. "At best, he would blast me off Olympus and take away my city. At worst, I would be put in Tartarus. But you must not let that distract you from your mission. You must be brave." He turned to the rest of the group. "You all must be brave. What you have faced so far is the easiest of your quest, but you cannot let the coming adversity make you lose sight of your goal."

Andy nodded. "I understand. But you still haven't answered my question about Darko."

Apollo's gaze fell to the forest floor as if in shame. "Alikan Village is gone. Destroyed. Every last satyr living there was slaughtered."

Zoey and Diana gasped, and Spencer's jaw dropped. Andy pressed his lips into a thin line. "How? How do you know that?"

"The satyrs thought they were keeping it a secret from us, the gods, but Zeus has known about it for a while. He had sent a few monsters their way, but they managed to defend their home with relatively few casualties. He came to the conclusion that he would need a group of demigods to destroy them, and originally planned to have Spencer, Karter, and Syrena do it, but obviously Syrena was sentenced to death, so that wasn't going to work. Right after he ordered Spencer and Karter to capture Diana, he had another team of demigods go to destroy the village."

Andy held back tears. He couldn't believe what he was hearing. "Why didn't you stop them? Why didn't you tell us?"

Apollo took a deep breath. "It happened yesterday. I found out today, and I hadn't had a chance to make myself present to you. But there was nothing I could have done to save them without jeopardizing my daughter's safety."

Spencer clenched his jaw. "Who did it? Who slaughtered the village?"

"It was Violet, Layla, and Xander," Apollo said. "But

it is none of your concern. They know nothing of your mission, and if you hurry, you can still make it to Hades on time."

Andy threw his hands in the air. "And what about Darko? Who's going to tell him what happened to the village?"

Diana rested a palm on his shoulder. "When we get back from Hades, we'll tell him."

Andy swallowed the lump in his throat. It didn't look as if they had another choice.

It was time to go to Hades.

~~*~

Screaming. It came from Karter's throat, deafening and spine tingling.

A ray of white light shone down on him, nothing but a black abyss beyond. His arms and legs were shackled with iron chains bolted to the ground.

He screamed for Spencer and Syrena. He screamed for Asteria. He screamed for his mother.

Soft footsteps pitter-pattered in the darkness before him, and a woman so beautiful and warm and kind it brought tears to his eyes stepped before him.

His mother.

She was just as he remembered. Soft and pale, with pale-blue eyes and long black hair. She wore a turquoise dress; turquoise had always been her favorite color. She gasped at the sight of him and rushed to his side, then pried the chains with her hands.

His heart calmed, his chest welling with grateful warmth. "Mom, I thought I'd never see you again."

She gritted her teeth, pulling at the chains. "I have to get you out of here, Karter."

His gaze traveled up the ray of light. "I'm okay. Now that I got to see you, I can die happy."

"No, you can't. Spencer needs your help!" she cried.

He jerked his head to look at her. "Why do you say that?"

She cupped his cheeks with soft hands, looking deep into his eyes. Images flashed inside her pupils, sucking him in.

He was on a beach, waves kissing the shore. The setting sun cast gorgeous shades of pink and purple and orange across the sky. Syrena skipped ahead of him, her curls flying in the wind. She dipped her hands in the saltwater and sprayed him with it, giggling. Spencer appeared on the other side of him and ran to her. He took her hand and pulled her into a passionate kiss.

Karter stuck his tongue out in mock disgust. They pulled away from each other and looked to Karter. "We love you too, Karter," Spencer said, laughing. They leapt toward him and grabbed his hands, then dragged him into the waves.

The image released him. He stared at his mother, his heart pounding. Worry lines creased her skin. "Spencer faces a battle in Hades, and if you don't break these chains and get there in time to save him, he will lose."

Karter's heart stopped. "So he'll die?"

"Yes. Just like Syrena."

Karter went numb. What was the point of living if everyone he cared about was dead? His mother, Syrena, and Spencer?

He clenched his fists and mustered all the strength in his body. He focused, focused, focused on breaking the chains. He yanked. Sweat rolled down his forehead. He screamed, veins bulging from his limbs. His vision went red. But the chains wouldn't budge.

"You must wake up," Asteria's familiar voice whispered. "Wake up, Karter."

Karter opened his eyes. Asteria hovered over him, cupping his cheeks with her hands. They were soft, so soft, like his mother's. "It is time for you to go to Hades," she said.

His limbs ached as though he'd really been chained to the ground, his knife wounds stinging. "He truly might die? You're sure?"

"Yes. I *am* a goddess of prophetic dreams, after all."

"How do I get there?"

"I will show you the way."

CHAPTER THIRTEEN

UNDERWORLD

Gray clouds hid the rising sun as the group flew toward Hades. Fog crept along the ground and all the way into the sky the farther they traveled, and Andy shivered from the cold, his teeth chattering.

He'd expected to see only forest below, but within the span of a few hours, they soared over the ruins of many old, forgotten towns. The roads were rubble, the buildings collapsed on top of each other. Bushes poked out of the debris, and trees stood guard around the city's perimeter. The sight of it all took Andy back to the moment he'd woken up to the destruction of his own town.

A few more hours passed, and the group entered an area that, even covered by dense fog, looked like the canyons of Utah. There were steep, jagged hills, and cliffs made of red-and-orange rock that went on farther than he could see. Sad little pine trees stuck out through the rocks, trying their best to grow.

They flew above the canyons for a while, a silent nervousness creeping through the air, before finally Spencer landed Ajax next to a rounded-off ten-foot-tall rock with a circle large enough for them to step into worn in the center.

Diana landed Aladdin next to him. They all climbed to the ground and readied their weapons. "We're here," Spencer said.

Zoey shivered. "This place is creepy."

Andy shrugged. "Well, it is the entrance to the underworld."

Diana turned to them, her expression stern. "My dad won't be there to help us this time. And my abilities will probably be weakened because we'll be so far away from the sun, so we'll have to be extra careful not to get hurt."

Andy eyed the entrance, dread filling his body. A week and a half ago he hadn't even known Greek gods were real, but now he was about to march into one's home and steal his magic hat. "Let's get this over with."

Diana smirked and gave Spencer a sideways glance. "You lead the way, Son of Hades."

Spencer turned to Ajax and Aladdin and stroked their noses. "Will you two wait here for us, please?" They snorted happily in response. With that he stepped into the entrance. As he passed through, his body morphed into a black shadow and disintegrated on the other side, like sand blowing away in the wind. Diana followed him, leaving Andy and Zoey last.

For a moment, they stared at each other. Zoey's eyes

were full of uncertainty, and Andy held his breath. What could they expect? What monsters awaited them now? What if their plan with Persephone didn't work, and they had to fight Hades? Were they strong enough to win? And if they were, did that mean Andy would be able to bring his family back from the dead?

Zoey stepped toward the entrance. Unsure of his own motives, Andy grabbed her hand and pulled her back. She swung around to look at him. He bit his lip. "Zoey, if we don't make it out of here, I just . . ." He leaned into her, his heart pounding. He'd never kissed a girl; he didn't know how all this worked. Was it all right to kiss her? How would she react?

Her cheeks turned pink, and for a moment, he doubted himself. He knew she had a crush on Spencer. She couldn't have feelings for him too. Could she?

He'd never know unless he confessed his own feelings.

He took a deep breath. This was it. He needed to tell her how he felt, how he'd always felt, in case this was the last time he'd have the chance.

She backed away from him but held tight to his hand. "You don't need to worry about that. We'll make it out." She turned around and stepped through the entrance, pulling him with her.

Every molecule in his body lit on fire, his ears ringing. His stomach churned violently, blurs of black-and-red flames scorching his pupils. Worst of all, he couldn't feel Zoey's hand in his anymore.

And then everything slowed down. The heat pulsing through his body cooled. His stomach calmed. His vision turned only to black, and fingers nervous with sweat squeezed his own. He blinked several times, trying to regain his composure, and the scene before him began to materialize, though his ears still rang.

The slanted walls of a cave spun around them like a barrel in a funhouse. Zoey was beside him, holding his hand, her cheeks a sick shade of green. Diana and Spencer were rushing to their sides. Andy grew dizzy watching them, nearly falling over. Spencer caught him by the waist and held him upright. Zoey dropped her axe and stumbled to the side, chunky puke spewing from her lips. Diana held her hair back, then wiped her mouth with the hem of her dress.

The walls stopped spinning. Everyone lurched backward and fell onto their butts. Andy rubbed his temples, and to his relief, his hearing returned to normal. The walls began to bubble, then morphed into a narrow stone hallway with a night-sky ceiling, where complete darkness waited for them at the end.

A woman cackled in the darkness ahead, her laughs bouncing off the walls. She stepped into the hall, tossing a golden apple back and forth between her hands. She was tall, with skin paler than a corpse, silky ebony hair, and piercing brown eyes. A plum dress clung to her skeletal body, a sinister grin plastered on her lips as a forked tongue slithered in and out of them. "Welcome to Hades," she said. "I'm not sure why the living continue to think they'll survive the trip, but welcome nonetheless."

Spencer bowed respectfully. "Hello there, Eris. Goddess of Chaos." Andy guessed the demigod greeted her like that for his and Zoey's benefit. "Very nice to see you again."

Eris stopped tossing the apple and snapped her bony fingers. "I thought I recognized you. Spencer, Son of Hades. I suspect you're not here for a friendly visit? I heard your girlfriend was sentenced to death. Trying to save her soul? Or are you here on some other *impossible* quest? Whatever it may be, I suggest you turn back. You're in between the land of the living and the land of the dead right now, but if you pass through the end of this hall and go across the Acheron, you won't have a way out. You'll be trapped forever, unless you have a way to convince Hades to let you out." She winked. "Or if some other god takes pity on you."

Diana stepped forward. "We're aware of where we are and what we're doing. Now move aside, please."

"Very well, I will go." She rested her gaze on Andy. "This will be so much fun to watch." As the words left her mouth, she slipped back into the shadows and left them in silence.

Andy shivered. Why did she have to look at *him* when she said that? It was totally creepy.

Spencer walked toward the end of the hallway, gesturing for them to follow. "C'mon. We have to keep moving."

Zoey retrieved her axe and caught up to Spencer. Andy slumped his shoulders in defeat. *So much for telling her how you feel*, he thought. Diana gave him a sad, knowing smile.

They reached the end of the hall and stepped into the dark. The ground beneath Andy's feet disappeared, and he fell through pitch-black, his stomach in his throat. Within seconds his feet hit a hard cave floor.

The cave was unlike anything he'd seen before, even Medusa's lair. It was huge; the ceiling had to be at least two hundred feet tall. A short walk ahead of them, a long river glowed red, licking back and forth, illuminating the spacious black walls. A cloaked figure rowing a rickety ferry came toward them in the distance.

"It's Charon," Spencer said. "Hopefully he'll accept our drachmas. He won't be very happy we didn't have a proper burial, or that Hermes didn't bring us here."

"How about the fact that we're not dead?" Andy said.

"That too."

Diana stepped toward the river and knelt before it. "This is the Acheron."

"River of Woe," Spencer said. "The bridge between the living and the dead."

The ground shook, and Andy stumbled back. The rocks shifted into wood, the whole of the ground into a dock, and the tremor stopped. Up ahead, the air around the ferry flickered, and when it returned to normal Charon was nearly to the dock, his face hidden under his cloak.

Andy hoped he'd let them cross. Otherwise their whole

journey would be for nothing, and he might never get to see his family again.

The ferry approached, slamming into the dock, and Andy was surprised it held together on impact, let alone stayed afloat. The wood looked as though it was decaying, holes throughout and bits of fungus trapped between the boards. The hood of Charon's cloak fell around his shoulders, revealing a pale man with sunken cheeks, long black hair, and startling red eyes. He pointed at them, his face twisted in a scowl. "None of you are dead. Turn back." His voice was like dead leaves rustling against each other. "Get out."

Spencer pulled the sack of drachmas from his robe and shelled out four of the silver coins. "Please, we need to get across the river."

"You're not dead. Only the dead go across."

"You can't make an exception?"

"Rules are rules."

Spencer pulled out two more drachmas and wiggled them in his fingers. "Please?"

Charon raised an eyebrow. "Why are you here?"

"We're here to save a friend," Diana said. "She was unfairly taken. It was too soon—"

Charon rolled his eyes. "That's what they all say. Everyone loses the people they love, and some are reckless enough to travel down here and try to bring them back. What do you think would happen if I just let everybody in and out as they pleased? It would be chaos. There would be no difference between the living and the dead."

Spencer pulled out two more drachmas. "Take us across, and I'll pay you double."

Charon smirked. "I suppose a little chaos wouldn't be so bad for that kind of payment." He snatched the coins from Spencer. "But you'll have to wait for a hearing with King Hades to consider resurrecting your friend. He's very busy, you know."

Spencer dumped the rest of the coins into Charon's boat in a heaping pile. "Don't tell a soul about our arrival, not even Hades, and you can have all of it."

Charon smiled with crooked yellow teeth. "You've got yourself a deal."

They climbed into the ferry, and Charon began to row them across. For a long time the group said nothing, instead gazing between the walls and each other in apprehension.

Zoey looked down at the river as it rocked the ferry back and forth. "Why is it called the River of Woe?"

"Mortals always assume it's a place of punishment," Charon said. "But in truth, it's a place of healing, of cleansing before judgment. Any mortals who dip themselves in it will be purged of their sins. Of course, the judges will remember the wrongs the mortals committed in life. But the mortals will be free of guilt for themselves." Zoey stared at the river as though she wanted to take a swim in it, but Andy had no idea why. She was a good person, one of the best people he knew.

He placed a hand on hers. "What's wrong?"

She pulled away and shook her head. "It's nothing." For the rest of the trip across the river, she stared at her palms, her gaze dull. Andy wished he knew what was wrong, or at least how to make her feel better.

After about an hour of rowing across the river, the group reached a long, narrow cavern lit by torches blazing with red fire. Dense fog crept across its floor, reaching toward the ferry.

Charon stopped rowing. "We've reached the end of the river."

A dock appeared beside them, and Diana rose, gathering her bow and arrows. "I never would have guessed." The group climbed out of the ferry and stepped onto the dock. Charon rowed away.

"Why do the drachmas work as a bribe for him?" Zoey asked, then gestured at their dismal surroundings. "It doesn't look like he has a place to use them."

"Oh, he does," Diana said. "Every couple of years he's allowed to leave Hades and go to either the winter or summer solstice party. During that time, he can use the drachmas he's collected to pay for whatever pleasurable things he wants. While he's gone, some other minor god has to take his place. It's the only way he doesn't go crazy and refuse to row souls across the Acheron, so the gods have always allowed it."

"I'd go crazy too if I had to do his job for thousands of years," Andy said.

They walked side by side into the narrow cavern, weapons drawn. "The gates to Hades should be at the end of this," Spencer said. "Guarded by Cerberus, the giant three-headed dog."

"And we'll have to fight him, right?" Zoey asked.

Spencer shrugged. "I'm not sure. He's supposed to let everyone in and no one out. But we're alive, so the same rules don't really apply to us."

Somewhere behind them, a little girl giggled, and Andy swung around in surprise. It was a muffled noise, but it sounded like . . . "Mel-Mel?" he called. Since his family was dead, had they gone to Hades?

Was this his chance to save them?

The group turned to him in concern, and he cupped his forehead. "I heard a little girl. It sounded like my sister . . ."

Spencer shook his head. "It couldn't be her. If she's in Hades, she'll be past the gates in one of the afterlives." Andy nodded and let out a deep breath. They pressed on.

After a few minutes of walking, the terrified scream of a young woman pierced the air from behind. A chill ran through Andy's spine. It sounded like Zoey . . .

He stopped, eyeing the others. Zoey was fine. She wasn't hurt, she wasn't screaming, and none of them seemed to have noticed a cry had gone through the cavern. He slowly turned around and looked back into the fog.

A familiar, sinister voice of a woman whispered in his ear, "I sense you've come for a battle." Eris materialized next to him. He said nothing, paralyzed with a rush of fear. "I sense you're all in danger." He shook his head and stepped backward, but she drew closer. "I sense that today, you all will *die*."

He spun around, darted toward the group, and crashed into Diana. She shrieked and stumbled forward. "Hey, watch it," she snapped.

Andy gulped, and they all turned to him, their expressions morphing from annoyance to concern. "What's wrong?" Zoey said.

"Eris—she—she said . . ."

Spencer put a hand on Andy's shoulder. "Don't listen to her. As the Goddess of Chaos, she's caused her fair share of problems throughout history." He glared at the shadows behind them. "Leave us alone, Eris." Andy glanced over his shoulder. Eris was gone, but her words lingered in his mind, filling him with a sense of dread. Spencer pulled away. "All right. Let's keep going."

Ahead of them a dog's howl echoed off the walls, and goose bumps rose on Andy's arms. "Please tell me you guys at least heard *that*," he said, tightening the grip on his sword.

The group exchanged fearful glances, and Diana nocked an arrow. "Oh, we did."

They tiptoed down the rest of the narrow cavern, the end opening to what seemed like a new realm. Black storm clouds clustered in a blood-red sky. Dense fog rolled along the ground. Thick bushes of twisting thorns led to and curled over diamond-encrusted gates, all the way into the eerie red glow beyond.

Andy shivered. "This place looks like a haunted cemetery."

The dog howled again. It barreled toward the gates from the other side, and Andy almost pissed his pants. It had to be at least fifteen feet tall, and where its tail should have been, a serpent writhed and hissed. Its three heads looked like pit bulls, their slobbering mouths lined with razor-sharp teeth, their eyes glowing red as the Acheron. Solid muscles rippled under its short gray coat, even more snakes poking out from random places in its fur.

"That's Cerberus," Spencer whispered. Cerberus jumped over the gates, and when his paws slammed into the ground, he shook the cavern, sending the group stumbling backward.

Zoey climbed to her feet. "Any idea how we're supposed to fight that thing and win?"

Diana scanned the cavern. "Heracles once captured him. But he was so strong he strangled Cerberus into submission. None of us have that kind of strength—we're just going to have to see if he'll let us pass."

"And if he doesn't?" Andy asked.

"Then we'll have to kill him and get past the gates before he regenerates himself," Spencer said. Andy exchanged a glance with Zoey, gulping, and she gave him an encouraging nod.

They tiptoed their way toward the gates. Cerberus eyed

them, his heads cocked in different directions.

When they reached the gates, Cerberus made his way toward them and blocked their path. One head licked its chops and gave them a puppy's grin, while the other two panted, their drool dripping onto the cavern floor. If Andy weren't afraid of him ripping off their heads, he might have thought he was cute.

"Think he's going to attack?" Diana asked, bow and arrow ready.

"I have no idea," Spencer said. "Let's just try to go in." He moved to Cerberus's left, ready to walk around the dog, but Cerberus extended a giant paw and blocked his path. He whined as if to say, *No, Mister. You don't want to go in there. Too scary.* Spencer brandished his spear. "Let us pass." Cerberus whined some more.

Zoey set her axe down and stepped toward the dog. Andy grabbed her shoulder. "What are you doing?"

She pulled away, a small smile on her lips. "I had a dog a long time ago. Her name was Daisy, and if our friend Cerberus here is anything like her, I know just the thing to get us past these gates." She rested her hands on Cerberus's paw and gently petted him, then began to hum a tune so soft and sweet Andy had trouble keeping from dozing off himself. Soon enough, Cerberus's heads and many snakes were swaying back and forth to her humming, his eyes closed. He curled up and started to snore.

Diana grinned. "Good job," she whispered.

Zoey grabbed her axe. "Thanks. Now we just need to

figure out a way over the gates."

"We can't open them and go through," Spencer said. "It will alert everyone in Hades that we're here."

Diana put her arrow back into her pack. "Then we'll just have to climb over." Andy sheathed his sword, and before he knew it they were sneaking up the gates, avoiding catching their hands or feet on the thorns.

On the other side, a blanket of fog and darkness dotted with precious gems went for miles. A line of people led toward a distant stone castle, thorns twisted all around it. They moaned and groaned. Smoke curled off their floating bodies.

The group climbed to the ground, and Andy raised his eyebrows. "Who are they?"

"The souls of the dead that haven't been judged yet," Spencer said.

"Is that where Hades lives?" Zoey asked, pointing at the castle.

"Yes," Spencer replied. "But we can't just waltz in there. We have to get past the judges first."

"And how are we supposed to do that?"

"We'll sneak around them."

The group slipped past the souls, staying in the shadows, occasional blood curdling screams echoing through the air.

After what seemed like forever they reached the front of the line, about a half mile away from the castle. Souls floated into a pillared black temple adorned with thorns and human bones. From inside, Andy heard the voices of men shouting, "Fields of Punishment!" and a woman begging for mercy.

No one exited the other side of the temple, and he imagined that with a snap of their fingers, the judges sent the souls to the afterlife they saw fit. The thought made him shiver, and he hoped that when he died, his soul would go to a more merciful place.

The group snuck around the temple, then dashed through the shadows toward the castle.

* ~ * ~ * ~

Asteria made a trail of stars all the way to Hades, and Karter followed them, flying until he reached the entrance.

His body ached, especially where he'd been sliced and stabbed, and he was covered in a disgusting mixture of blood and sweat. His chest burned hotter than ever, and he'd used almost all his strength, but he pressed on. He had to reach Spencer before it was too late.

Two pegasi at the entrance neighed at him, trying to block his path, but he shoved past them. The portal consumed his body. His stomach churned, and when he reached a spinning cave he retched, swaying back and forth from dizziness.

The cave transformed into a night-sky hallway, and Eris waited for him at the end. "Karter, Son of Zeus, what a pleasure. Come to help your friend?" She licked her lips.

"Don't bother, you're too late."

Karter wiped his mouth. "Let me through."

Eris cackled and stepped aside. "Very well then. More fun for me."

* ~ * ~ * ~

Once the group barged through the front doors of the castle, Andy understood exactly why Persephone hated her time in the underworld.

The rooms were made with cold gray stone and lit with dim candlelight, and they smelled like thousand-year-old mildew. Hundreds of smiling skulls lined the walls, and all the furniture—the chairs, the tables, the couches—was crafted from human bones and glittering jewels. The wide, arched windows gave a view of the black storm clouds and blood-red sky outside, framed with tattered curtains that looked as if moths feasted on them daily. Worst of all, the castle was silent. So silent all Andy could hear were his own shallow breaths and the pattering of the group's footsteps.

Spencer led them as they raced through the halls, before finally, they stumbled into the throne room.

It was cave-like, with high ceilings and wide walls lined with skulls, precious gems lodged everywhere. A long red rug led down the center of the room to a dais with two thrones, a black curtain suspended behind them. The larger throne was made of charred bones and shimmering diamonds, the smaller made of brown vines and wilted wildflowers.

Between the thrones, atop a pedestal of bone, sat a helmet the color of charcoal, with swirling designs carved all over it. Although it was normal in appearance, ancient power emanated from it as though it were a god itself.

Zoey stepped toward the helmet, reaching for it. "Whoa. Is that the Helm of Darkness?"

From behind the curtain, the oily voice of a man said, "Yes, it is. Now, would you four like to tell me why you're sneaking about in *my* castle?"

Andy shivered. *Guess Persephone couldn't help us after all*, he thought.

Hades lifted the curtain and stepped before them. He was thin and tall, almost seven feet, with a commanding presence. His cheeks were so pale and gaunt he looked as if he needed an eternal supply of sunlight and cheeseburgers. His dark hair was slicked back as though he'd combed it with olive oil, and he wore floor-length heavy black robes with jewels embedded in the fabric. Power seemed to roll off him, much like the Helm.

Spencer brandished his spear. "Father, what a pleasure to see you again."

"Why have you come here, my son?" Hades said, picking up the Helm and tucking it under his arm. "I know of your mission to capture the Daughter of Apollo, and yet now she seems to be your ally." He narrowed his eyes at Andy and Zoey. "And who are these two? They reek of worthless mortal."

"Don't underestimate them," Spencer hissed.

Hades laughed. "Are you joking? Son, please, explain yourself. Have you come to save Syrena's soul? Is that what this is all about? You must know I will never let her go. Not after her betrayal of the gods."

Spencer clenched his jaw. "What have you done with her?"

Hades grinned and licked his lips. "Why, I've given her the worst punishment possible. She burns in the fires of Tartarus, with the likes of the Titans."

Diana gasped, her eyes filling with tears, and Spencer lunged for Hades. "No!" he cried.

Hades sidestepped Spencer and kicked him face-first to the ground. He drew a dagger from his robes, and Andy, Zoey, and Diana rushed forward, weapons ready for battle.

"You know I don't want to hurt you, my son," Hades said. "Truly, I care for you. But I will do what I must to assure all demigods stay in line."

"And I'll do whatever it takes to see the gods burn in Tartarus," Spencer spat.

Hades snarled and raised his dagger, but before the fight could begin, a short young woman in ancient Greek armor—complete with sword, helmet, and shield— stepped out from the curtain and stabbed Hades in the back.

Hades sucked in a short breath and dropped his dagger. The young woman ripped the sword from his back and raised it above her head, then swung it through the god's neck. His head fell to the floor next to her feet. His body collapsed, and glowing gold liquid pooled around him from his wounds. The Helm rolled out of his grasp, clanking against the floor. She kicked his head across the room.

Spencer climbed to his feet and turned to the girl. "Persephone?"

She nodded and removed her helmet, chestnut-brown hair falling over her shoulders. "I apologize for taking so long." Her hazel eyes glittered with excitement. "You have no idea how long I've wanted to do that."

Spencer smiled and turned to Andy and Zoey. "Quickly now, one of you get the Helm. We need to leave before Hades regenerates himself."

Zoey reached for the Helm with her free hand, but Persephone shoved her away and grabbed the Helm for herself, then slipped back toward the curtains.

Spencer faced Persephone, brow furrowed. "What are you doing?"

Persephone laughed, sheathed her sword, and tucked the Helm under her arm. "I've been waiting for this moment since I discovered you were born, Spencer."

"What are you talking about?" Spencer asked, his voice shaking.

Persephone snapped her fingers, and the piercing screeches of women echoed off the walls from behind. Andy looked over his shoulder, and three ugly women wielding whips flew into the room. They wore all red, their wings black and leathery. Green serpents were entwined around their arms and waists and through their greasy hair. They glided above the group, then landed behind Persephone.

"The Furies," Diana said. "Goddesses of vengeance and retribution."

Spencer's eyes widened. "I thought the Furies served Hades."

"We serve both King Hades and Queen Persephone," one said. "But now, Queen Persephone holds the Helm of Darkness. She rules the underworld."

Persephone giggled, twirling her hair through her fingers. "I've always hated you, Spencer. You're the child of my husband from another woman."

"But you don't love Hades," Spencer said. "He kidnapped you. He forced you to marry him."

She smirked. "But with time I fell in love with him. And, for the most part, he stayed loyal to me, unlike the other gods to their wives. Until he met your mother at a summer solstice party held on Olympus."

"Yeah, I already know that story," Spencer said. "He met my mother, and I was conceived. He went back to Hades, and you helped her give birth to me. She died after I was born, her last wish that I be named after her father, Spencer. And you brought me here and helped raise me."

"Hades and I never told you the full story," Persephone chirped. "He loved your mother, as he loved me when we first married. But he didn't have to kidnap her. She willingly came here with him, and when I returned for the fall and winter months, he hid her from me. But soon you were born, and I discovered their affair. As punishment, I took your mother to the River Lethe and forced her to drink from it."

Spencer's lip quivered. "The River of Forgetfulness."

"Yes," Persephone said. "She forgot all about you, and all about Hades."

"What did you do to her?"

"I set her free in the forest. Of course, eventually, monsters found and ate her."

A tear rolled down Spencer's cheek. "Why have you waited this long to betray me? You had so many chances to kill me while I was growing up."

"Your father protected you and swore he would put me in Tartarus if I hurt you," she replied, laughing. "That was when I fell out of love with him, and with each day my hatred for him grew. I decided that one day I would rule the underworld myself and kill you. I wanted to wait for you to grow up so I could watch you suffer. After all, the path paved for demigods is a path of misery and heartbreak. When you came to me for help into Hades, well, it was the perfect opportunity to not only take this place for myself, but also to lure you into my trap. You'd suffered the greatest loss you ever could. Your dearest love, Syrena, had just been put to death. And your best friend, the young demigod you have many a time called your brother, abandoned you to fight for her alone."

From behind, the familiar voice of a young man said, coughing, "I may have left him to fight alone before, but I'm here now." They swung around, and there was Karter, floating to the floor. He clutched his side, his face drawn in pain, blood trickling from his wounds.

Spencer's jaw dropped. "Karter?"

Hades's head snaked back toward his body, but Persephone stopped it with her foot before they could reunite. "I'd love to stay and ramble on, but I really do need to dispose of this." She slipped the Helm of Darkness on, and her body disintegrated into the shadows. She picked up the head, which disappeared with her, and burst into a fit of laughter.

Spencer leapt toward where she'd stood and jabbed his spear at the air. "You're a monster!" he shouted. She yelped, and the Helm fell off. She reappeared and stumbled to the floor, Hades's head still tucked under her arm.

The Furies snarled and leapt into the air toward the group. Andy slashed the first in her ugly face, and Zoey hacked at her limbs. Diana sent arrows flying at the second, and even Karter joined the group, launching two lightning bolts toward the third.

Spencer lunged for Persephone. She kicked his spear out of his grasp and jumped to her feet. She unsheathed her sword and, before Spencer could retrieve his weapon, plunged the blade through his stomach and twisted it upward.

"Spencer!" Zoey yelped. Andy tried to run to the demigod's side, but a Fury knocked his sword from his hand and shoved him to the ground.

Spencer cried out. Persephone ripped the sword from his abdomen. She snatched the Helm and put it on, then disappeared into the shadows. "Furies, kill the intruders."

CHAPTER FOURTEEN

APPLES

Andy's thoughts raced, his heart pounding. Persephone had betrayed them, taken the Helm, and run off into the castle with it. Spencer had been stabbed in the gut. Not to mention Eris had predicted they'd all die in Hades, and a Fury had knocked Andy's weapon aside and pinned him to the ground.

It just wasn't that great of a day. Not that any day over the course of the last eleven days had been particularly swell.

The Fury dug her nails into his shoulders. She picked him up and slammed his skull against the floor, knocking his glasses off his head. "This is how you die, mortal," she hissed in his face, the scent of rotting flesh on her breath.

Andy's vision spun. "The gods really should issue everyone mouthwash or something." His skull cracked against the floor. He gritted his teeth. "Honestly, you don't even need to be violent. You could just breathe on us and that'd get the job done." She roared in his face.

Golden electricity whizzed over his head and blasted the Fury in the chest. She screeched and let go of him, then fell back. He snatched his glasses, put them back on, and rubbed his temples, swaying from dizziness.

His vision cleared just enough so that he could make out what was happening, and he spotted Karter blasting lightning bolts at the Fury who'd attacked him. Who knew the guy had a moral compass? Diana sent spheres of light at another Fury's head, as she was out of arrows, and Zoey swung her axe at the last.

Agonized screams echoed off the walls, a sudden burst of wind whipping Andy's hair back and forth. Bones from all over the room tore themselves from their places: the walls, the throne, the pedestal. They floated toward Spencer, who was sprawled on the ground with his hands raised. The bones clattered against each other, bobbing up and down and cracking into place until they'd formed a small army of six skeletons.

They looked to Spencer. "Go," he rasped. "Save my friends, and kill the winged women."

The skeletons rolled their jaws, moaning and groaning as they advanced toward the Furies. They tackled the Furies in groups of two, then pulled them by their leathery wings away from Karter, Diana, and Zoey. The Furies wailed, slapping whips against the skeletons' skulls, but the skeletons pulled them to the ground.

One Fury escaped the skeletons' grasps, and Diana blasted a sphere of light at her head. Chunks of bone and brains splattered everywhere. The Fury's body sailed onto the floor. The last two Furies writhed against the skeletons, trying to escape, but the skeletons chomped and clawed their flesh. Soon they were torn apart in a pile of golden blood and guts.

Once the Furies were defeated, the skeletons collapsed into a heap of bones, whatever magical force holding them together lifting.

Diana and Zoey rushed to Spencer's side. Blood pooled around him. Karter kept his distance, watching them with a worried look. "Don't worry, I'll heal you," Diana assured him. Her breaths were labored and sweat rolled down her face, but still she lit her hands with gold light.

Andy tried to stand, but a wave of nausea and dizziness crashed through his body, and he collapsed. "Andy!" Zoey cried, running to his side. She examined his head and brushed his hair with her fingers. When she lifted her hand, blood coated them. "Your head—you're bleeding." Andy groaned, his vision growing blurrier by the second.

"Diana, you need to heal Andy," Spencer said.

"I'm not sure I have enough strength left for the both of you. Not until we get out of here."

"Then we'll worry about me later. Just, please . . . Heal him."

Warm light flooded Andy's body, and within a few moments, his vision returned to normal. Diana hovered over him, hyperventilating, every pore on her body seeping with sweat.

"Is he okay?" Spencer asked from across the room, his voice shaking.

Andy sat up. "I am." They crawled to Spencer's side.

Zoey took Spencer's hands. Her eyes filled with tears. "Are you going to be okay?"

He smiled, but his eyes were pained. He'd always looked so strong, so capable, but now, lying on the floor and soaked with blood, he looked weak, fragile. "Don't worry about me. Worry about getting the Helm."

Diana rubbed her forehead. "I'm not sure I can even walk now." She looked to Andy and Zoey, the green of her eyes dim. "You guys will have to fight Persephone alone."

Panic rose in Andy's chest. Not only was Persephone a goddess, but now she had one of the most powerful objects in existence, which also made her invisible. It was hopeless. "How are we supposed to fight her without you? We've barely been trained."

"I'll go with you," Karter said from behind them. He came forward and knelt next to Diana at Spencer's side. "I've been weakened from the trip here, and from fighting the Furies, but I'll do whatever it takes to help. I don't care what it is, as long as Spencer lives."

"What about the seeds she gave us?" Zoey asked. "Do you think they'll get us out of Hades?"

Spencer shook his head. "No. I'm sure they'd either kill us or trap us here forever. Diana and I will try to figure something else out."

Zoey squeezed Spencer's hands. "What if while we're

gone the Furies regenerate and attack you? What if some-one else figures out you're in the castle and hurts you?"

Diana reached over and cupped Zoey's cheek with her palm. "You can't worry about that right now. Just worry about getting the Helm so you can fight the gods."

Zoey choked on her breath, surely holding back tears, and Andy rested a hand on her back. "All right," she said.

Spencer coughed. "Persephone said she was going to dispose of Hades's head. The only place she could get rid of it without it making its way back to his body and re-generating is Tartarus. Go out the other end of the castle, through the Fields of Elysium, Asphodel, and Punish-ment. The pit of Tartarus is at the very end of the Fields of Punishment, but you have to be careful not to let it suck you in."

Andy, Zoey, and Karter nodded and gathered their weapons, then ran toward the other end of the castle.

They wove through dark halls and past winding stair-cases, finally reaching a large window with a view of para-dise. Rays of bright light poked through the fluffy clouds of its blue sky, and green hills rolled along the landscape. Leafy trees and colorful flowers swayed in a breeze. White palaces glittered. Men and women danced along the grass, adorned with golden robes and jewelry.

"Elysium," Karter said, and sent a sandaled foot through the glass of the window. It shattered, and shards littered the floor. He held his hands out to Andy and Zoey. "If we want to catch Persephone, we need to fly."

Andy and Zoey exchanged an uncomfortable glance, and Karter sighed. "I don't expect you to trust me, and obviously I'm not doing this for you or your cause. I'm doing it for Spencer. But if you want to succeed, if you want him to live, you're going to have to do what I say." They took Karter's hands. He pulled them against his chest and leapt into the clouds.

It didn't take long to fly through Elysium's crisp, fresh air, and soon they passed across chilly mountains with snowcapped peaks. On the other side of the mountains, hordes of people with confused looks on their faces shuffled through what seemed to be an unending field of dead grass. The air was stuffy, like the inside of a basement closet, the sky a gloomy gray.

"Asphodel," Karter said.

It took triple the time it took to pass through Elysium to pass through Asphodel, and eventually they reached a cluster of giant black spikes reaching for the clouds. Once they passed them, they entered a place no one would want to spend the rest of eternity.

Terrible screaming filled the red sky. The smell of smoke and burnt flesh scorched the air. The hills were made of black soil and rocks, volcanoes scattered across them and bubbling with glowing lava, charred bones and flames climbing from the cracks. Chains locked various people to the ground, their backs lashed by faceless men in dark cloaks. Others hung by their necks on leafless trees, while some were dipped in and out of the volcanoes. Andy caught sight of a man being chopped to pieces, sewn back together, then chopped up again. He shivered, looking away.

"The Fields of Punishment," Karter said. "We're getting close to Tartarus."

When the screaming grew quiet, Andy decided it was safe to look again, but was filled with dread at what he saw. Below them, there were miles of black soil. In the distance a giant pit awaited them, an abyss as wide as New York and deep as the ocean, blue flames licking like waves at its edge. Gusts of wind blew into it, as though it were sucking in one deep, eternal breath.

Karter descended, his breathing shallow. They reached the ground, and he released them from his grasp. "We're here." He pointed at the pit with a shaking hand. "That's Tartarus."

Andy's feet crunched against the dirt, and as they walked toward Tartarus, faint tracks were left in their wake.

"Persephone can't fly, right?" Andy said. "She must have left some tracks."

Zoey nodded. "That's what I was thinking. Just because she's invisible doesn't mean she wouldn't leave a trail."

"Unless she transported herself here," Karter said. "She's in her element right now, so she's most powerful, and could probably send herself anywhere in the underworld within a few seconds."

"Even still, would she have transported herself straight to the edge?" Zoey replied. "I know she's a powerful goddess, but from what I've heard about Tartarus, I doubt she wants to fall in."

They crept across the dark plain, scanning the ground for any sign of her tracks, fighting against the wind in silence as it tried to suck them in, but found nothing.

Andy clutched his sword with white knuckles. As scared as he was, he wanted to destroy Persephone, especially for what she'd done to Spencer. She pretended to love him, pretended to be a good mother figure, then revealed she'd wiped his birth mother's memory, killed her, and plotted his death until she got the chance to strike. She was totally evil.

Plus, he wanted Spencer to be okay. The guy left behind all he'd ever known to help them, did everything he could to train and protect them, and even after what could be a fatal injury, told Diana to heal Andy instead of himself. Granted, it was probably because Andy and Zoey were the key to the prophecy, but still, Andy appreciated it more than he could put into words. It was something he'd only do for the people he loved.

"There," Zoey said, pointing to the left. "I see some tracks." Sure enough, a line of tracks made by feet so dainty they could only belong to Persephone trailed toward the pit.

Andy braced himself. This was it. They neared the end, where they'd either retrieve the Helm and save the day, or fail and be thrown into the flames of Tartarus.

They followed the trail until it appeared the tracks had

stopped and turned around. They paused, the crunching of a fourth pair of feet ahead. New footsteps came toward them. Andy and Zoey raised their weapons while Karter readied his fists.

Persephone giggled. It was light and airy, a sound too sweet for a scheming, vengeful goddess. Andy held his breath. "I'm surprised to see you survived the Furies," she said. "That's an incredible feat, really. If you've come to get Hades, don't bother. I've already thrown his head into the pit." The blade of her sword *schwing*ed. "But, oh, what's this? Where's my pathetic stepson and the Daughter of Apollo? Did *they* survive?" Her tone was mocking.

Andy opened his mouth to reply, but before he could say a word, Zoey snarled and charged toward Persephone's tracks. She brought her axe down against them, and it sank into the soil. Andy and Karter rushed forward to help.

As they reached Zoey's side, there was a sickening *slice*—the sound of a blade tearing through flesh. Zoey let out a scream so awful it sent chills through Andy's body. She raised her right arm, her expression drawn in terror. Where her hand had once been, only a stump of skin and muscle and bone was left, blood squirting from it like a high-powered fountain. Her axe—and her hand, detached from her body—rolled off to the side and tumbled into the pit.

Andy knelt next to Zoey, unable to breathe. Persephone had hurt her. Persephone had *cut off her hand*. There was blood, so much blood. How was Zoey supposed to fight without her axe and with only one hand against an invisible attacker?

What if this was it? What if they'd never make it back to Spencer and Diana? What if they all died in this awful place? What if he never got the chance to tell Zoey how he felt about her? What if this meant he would lose the opportunity to save his best friend and family, and they had died in vain all those years ago? He'd never get to see them again, never get to hold them again, and for what?

Karter tore off the sleeve of his robes and wrapped it around Zoey's bloody stump. Once he finished, he stood, conjured a gold bolt, and chucked it toward more tracks. It only blasted the black soil. Zoey sobbed and clutched her arm.

"You're fighting for the wrong side," Persephone said. "Join me, all of you, and I can assure you you'll live to see another day. We'll steal Poseidon's Trident. We'll steal the Lightning Bolt. Together, we'll take down the Olympians, and I'll rule as your queen. Queen of the world."

Karter stood and made another bolt. "Never." He sent it through the air toward the tracks, but again, it didn't hit Persephone. The goddess cackled.

Zoey clenched her jaw. "Even if it means I die, I won't join you. Spencer loved you like a mother, and you betrayed him. You're disgusting."

"And what will you do when your little friend here accepts my proposition?" Persephone said. "His name is Andy, correct?"

"I never said I would," Andy said. "And I won't. Not now, not ever."

"Is that so, little boy?" Persephone chirped. "What if I told you that if you join me, as Queen of the Underworld, I could reunite you with your loved ones lost? With your best friend. Your mother, your sister. Your *father*."

Andy gasped, a lump in his throat. Was this what the Fates had meant when they'd said he'd have the opportunity to save his family if he went to Hades? "You mean . . . you'd bring them back to life?" he whispered.

Persephone laughed. "Oh, yes. With a combination of my own powers and the power of the Helm, it would be easy."

Andy gulped. His heart pounded, his body trembling. Was fighting Persephone truly worth it? What if joining her was his only chance to see his family again?

Zoey spat at Persephone's tracks. "Liar!" She turned to Andy, shaking her head, her eyes pleading with him. "Please, Andy, don't listen to her. Don't do it."

He thought of all the late nights he'd spent playing video games with Mark, of all the lazy afternoons he'd watched cartoons with Melissa. He thought of his mother as she worked tirelessly to give them a better life, of all the times she'd come home with dark bags under her eyes and a huge pile of homework, yet still managed to smile and make dinner. He thought of all the time he could have spent with his father. Of the many nights he'd sat awake, wanting and needing his guidance. Death had taken him far too early.

But then he thought of Vanessa. How he'd promised to protect her, and lost her to the Stymphalian Birds. He thought of Darko, of Diana, of Zoey. He thought of Spencer as Persephone stabbed him in the gut.

Fate was cruel.

He climbed to his feet, consumed with panic and anger and grief. He scanned the ground for fresh footprints with tears in his eyes and spotted them several feet ahead. Unsure of his own actions, he charged toward the footprints. They dodged his advances. He swerved toward them head-on, and something hit his shoulder.

No, something went *through* his shoulder. Warm, sticky blood soaked his shirt. The shock of it made him drop his sword, and the pit sucked it in. But he couldn't let that stop him. He had to get the Helm from Persephone.

With his free hand, he clawed his invisible attacker, seizing her by the wrist. Her blade plunged farther into his shoulder, electric tingles arcing through his body from the wound. He clenched his jaw and, using all the strength he could muster, wrestled her to the ground. The Helm rolled off her head and tumbled toward the pit of Tartarus, Persephone finally revealed.

"Zoey, grab the Helm!" Andy cried. She intercepted it with her hand and pulled it close to her chest.

Persephone's nostrils flared. She twisted the sword in Andy's shoulder. He screamed, searing heat flooding his body, his vision fading between red and black. A pair of arms tore him off her. The blade was ripped from his body, leaving only the heat.

His vision cleared. Persephone advanced toward Zoey, bloody sword in hand, as she scrambled backward.

"Zoey!" Andy cried. He tried to climb to his feet, but intensely hot, sharp pain shot from the wound. He fell to his knees.

Beside him, Karter conjured a gold bolt. Persephone reached Zoey, raising her blade. Karter chucked the bolt toward them. It soared through the air, then hissed as it hit Persephone's head. Her sword fell. She tumbled to the side in a daze. She took hold of Zoey's collar, dragging her with. They skidded toward the fiery pit.

"*No!*" Andy screamed. Karter flew after them, reaching for Zoey. She stretched her hand toward his.

He grabbed her by the fingertips and kicked Persephone off her, then pulled her tight to his chest and veered backward. The blue flames of the pit rose, swallowing the goddess, and she wailed. Wind tugged at Karter and Zoey, trying to suck them into the pit, but Karter pressed on. He flew to Andy's side.

Andy clutched his shoulder. "Zoey, thank God you're okay . . . I thought for sure you . . . you . . ." She stepped away from Karter and fell to her knees, then threw her arms around Andy's neck. He sucked in a deep breath and buried his hands in her curls.

She pulled out of their embrace and held up the Helm. "We have to get back to the castle," she said, her voice strained with pain.

Karter picked them up and flew them back. Andy held on with what little strength he had left, slipping in and out of consciousness. Even after they reached the castle, Karter kept them in his grasp.

Once they reached the throne room, Karter let them down at Spencer's side. He gasped for breath, sweat pooling down his body. He collapsed alongside them.

"We have the Helm," Andy said. "Hades and Persephone are in Tartarus."

Diana clutched her chest. "Zoey, you lost your hand? And Andy . . ."

"I was stabbed," he said with a weak chuckle.

Spencer's skin was pale and ashen. Blood trickled from his lips. "You two have done well. I'm so proud of you."

Andy shrugged, then winced at the pain in his shoulder. "We couldn't have done it without Karter. If he hadn't helped us out, we'd be dead." Spencer and Karter locked eyes, a sad expression passing between them.

Zoey dropped the Helm and grabbed Spencer's hand. "Did you find a way to get us out of here?" Spencer broke into a fit of bloody coughing. Diana pressed her lips into a thin line and shook her head. "So all of it was for nothing?" Zoey said. "We're just going to die here?"

The familiar cackle of a woman echoed off the walls, and from a shadowed corner, Eris stepped into the room before them. She licked her lips with her forked tongue and looked to Andy. "As I told you earlier, your quest was doomed, and you would surely die."

He hung his head in defeat. "I guess you were right."

She smirked. "What if I could help you succeed in your quest? What if I could help you out of Hades?"

"Please, help us," Andy said. "I'll do anything. Anything." And he meant it. If he had to cut off his own fingers, if he had to gouge out his own eyes, if he had to throw himself into Tartarus, he'd do it. As long as all this hadn't been in vain.

Eris laughed. "This will be so much fun to watch." She snapped her fingers, and with a flash of purple light, a brown drawstring sack appeared in her hands. She tossed it toward Andy. "These apples are full of magic, and one bite will return you to the living realm. *Only one bite*. They cannot be cut apart, cannot be shared, or they will lose their power. Know this: all gifts come with a price." She disappeared in a cloud of black smoke.

Andy tore open the bag to find four shiny gold apples.

"What did she give you?" Diana asked.

"They're apples," he said, grinning ear to ear. He handed Zoey, Diana, and Spencer each one, then took the last for himself. "If we eat them, we'll get out of here."

"What about Karter?" Spencer rasped, coughing. "Is there a fifth apple?"

Andy's heart sank. *All gifts come with a price.*

Karter shook his head. "It's okay, Spencer. It's okay. Just . . . get out of here. I'll be fine. I'll find another way."

"But you're dying," Spencer said. "You were sliced up

before any of us, and you've been losing blood this whole time. You flew all the way here, fought the Furies, then flew Zoey and Andy to Tartarus and back."

Karter smiled with quivering lips. "I came here to save you. Once you eat that apple, you'll escape, and Diana will heal you. You'll be okay. I've done what I set out to do."

Spencer sat up, grunting and groaning. "No." He shoved his apple toward Karter. "Take it."

"I refuse," Karter said, balling his fists. "I won't let you die because of me. Syrena already did."

Spencer smiled. "I'm not afraid of death anymore." His eyes glazed over. "S-Syrena . . ." He let out a final pained sigh, then fell onto his back. His apple rolled out of his hand and onto the floor.

Andy's breath caught in his throat. Karter stared aghast at Spencer. Diana covered her mouth in silent shock, and Zoey began to sob.

Diana reached over and checked Spencer for a pulse. She held back a strangled cry, then closed his eyes. "It's time to go."

"No," Zoey whimpered. She dropped her apple and grabbed Spencer's limp hand. "I won't leave him."

Diana trembled, her eyes brimming with tears. "He's gone. We have to."

"Isn't there a way to bring him back?" Andy asked, his voice cracking in desperation. "I mean, he hasn't been dead long. If gods and monsters and all this other bullshit exists, there has to be a way to save him."

"No," Diana replied. "No mortal can beat death, not unless the gods choose to raise their soul and give them immortal life. If there was a way to save him, you know I'd do it. But there's not. He's gone." Andy bit his lip. Tears gushed down his cheeks, a heavy ache in his chest.

Diana retrieved Zoey's apple. She tore Zoey's hand from Spencer's and shoved the apple into it. "We have to leave. You and Andy are hurt. If we wait much longer, you could die, or someone could find us here and figure out what's happened."

"How can you be so heartless?" Andy said.

Diana pounded her fist against the floor. "This is what Spencer would want!" Andy and Zoey quieted. Diana grabbed Spencer's apple and offered it to Karter. "He wanted you to have this, so you better take it. You can come with us if you'd like. After all, you helped steal the Helm."

Karter accepted the apple, but his gaze never left Spencer's body. "I can't leave him. Not yet."

Diana snatched her bow and swung her pack of arrows onto her back. Andy assumed she'd gathered them while he and Zoey fought Persephone, in case they were attacked again. "I guess we'll see you around." She lifted her apple to her lips. "All right, you two. Get the Helm." Andy grabbed it and tucked it under his arm. "On the count of three, we take a bite and leave this place." Andy sniffled, and Zoey burst into a fit of sobs. "One. Two. Three."

Andy took a bite.

CHAPTER FIFTEEN

RUNAWAY

The group appeared outside the entrance to Hades, a peaceful sunset near its end.

Zoey cried in despair, from both Spencer's death and from the blinding, white-hot pain of her lost hand. She collapsed face-first onto the ground, slipping into unconsciousness. Violent visions of winged women, the glimmering Helm, and her hand as it tumbled into the blue fire of Tartarus plagued her mind.

When she finally woke, a warm campfire crackled, thick pine trees overhead.

She gasped and sat upright. "What happened? What's going on?"

Andy snored from across the fire. Diana pushed a serving of meat and berries toward her. "Eat and go back to sleep. It's my turn to watch for monsters. In the morning, we'll get back to Deltama Village, properly rest, and form our next plan." Zoey's pain had lifted. She looked down. Her hand was still gone, but a fresh layer of skin covered the stump. "I'm sorry. That's all I could do for your hand," Diana said and turned away.

Zoey swallowed hard. Any hunger she may have felt vanished. She ignored the food and stared at the sky for the rest of the night, wondering how she was supposed to fight without her hand, and thinking of the night Spencer showed her her father's death and held her as she sobbed.

The next day, Diana gave Andy a brief lesson on how to direct a pegasus, and they rode Aladdin and Ajax back to Deltama Village. When they arrived, a few dozen villagers greeted them with excited chatter, and the pegasi disappeared into the crowd.

Kali ran toward the group. "Were you able to steal the Helm of Darkness?" Andy held the Helm up for all to see, and the villagers cheered. "Where's Spencer?" she asked, her voice laced with concern.

"He's dead," Diana said plainly, then choked on a sob. Kali rushed to her side and pulled her into a long embrace. Diana cried in her arms. Andy hung his head.

The reminder of Spencer's passing made Zoey burst into tears. He'd understood her, and was probably the only person in the world she wouldn't have been scared to tell more about her past. After all, he'd figured a lot of it out all on his own. Not to mention he'd helped her find the missing piece of it. She didn't think he would have developed any sort of crush or romantic feelings for her, like she had for him, but it didn't matter. He was her friend. And friends like Spencer didn't come by often. At least not for Zoey.

Darko pushed through the crowd, a smile on his face. "You're back. And you got the Helm. Does this mean we're going to Alikan Village?" Zoey wiped her tears, her stomach sinking as she remembered the village of satyrs Andy promised they'd take Darko to had been slaughtered. "Where's Spencer?"

Andy looked up. "Darko—there's—there's some things we have to tell you. First of all . . . Spencer is dead. Persephone betrayed us in Hades, and she killed him." Darko gasped. "And the second thing—you have to know, we didn't find this out until right before we had to go to Hades—well, everyone in Alikan Village was slaughtered a few days ago. The whole place was destroyed."

"No," Darko said. "That can't be."

"The gods had their eye on the village for a long time," Andy continued. "They sent monsters after the people there, but the villagers managed to defeat them. So Zeus sent a team of three demigods to the village with orders to—to kill everyone. And they succeeded."

Darko trembled. "Who told you that?" he asked, his voice cracking. "It has to be a lie."

"It's not. Apollo himself told us. I'm so sorry."

"No—no. After everything Phoenix did to . . ." Darko's eyes filled with tears. Andy stepped toward him and pulled him into a tight hug. He wept.

By nightfall, a few villagers had prepared the group dinner, although this time they opted to eat in Chief Agni's cabin rather than have a grand party.

As they ate, Zoey and Diana sat together on a fluffy couch, while Andy and Darko were sprawled out on a woven rug. Chief Agni stood, arms crossed, in front of the fire. Kali poked her food with a wooden spoon in a chair close to Diana.

"So, you lost your sword and axe," Chief Agni said, looking to Andy, then Zoey. They nodded. "We have a few spare spears. Would you like to take them when you leave, so you may have something to use until you're able to find more weapons?"

Zoey thought of the visions Spencer had shared with them. In every one, he'd used a spear. Even with her severed hand, she was sure to get the hang of using one in combat in no time because of that. "That would be wonderful. Thank you."

"We will send you with pegasi, of course," Chief Agni added. "And what of you, Darko? I know your village was destroyed. You are welcome to stay here if you'd like."

Darko shook his head. "Thank you for the offer, but I think I'd like to go with my friends, if they'll let me." Diana nodded, while Zoey and Andy gave him smiles.

Kali cleared her throat. "Father, they've lost a crucial member of their team. We should send them with a great warrior. Obviously no one could replace Spencer, but I'm sure they'll need an extra helping hand on their quest."

Chief Agni raised an eyebrow. "And who do you suggest we send, my daughter?"

All eyes were on Kali. "Well, I was thinking that . . . I could go. I could help them," she said.

The chief narrowed his eyes. "Absolutely not."

Diana set aside her empty plate and climbed to her feet. "No way, Kali. It's too dangerous for you to go. You've been living in this village your whole life."

Kali rolled her eyes. "Is that what you said to Andy and Zoey when you plucked them from the past, Princess?" Diana opened and closed her mouth several times, unable to come back with a clever retort. "Besides, I'm far from helpless. It's not like this place has been immune to attacks. I've killed a monster or two."

Chief Agni strode to Kali's side and rested a hand on her shoulder. "Whether or not you're a capable enough warrior to go with them is not the issue. In fact, there's no doubt in my mind that you are. But I won't have you risking your life for something that isn't your responsibility. You're too important—to me, and to our village."

Kali averted her gaze to the floor, as if in defeat. "All right, Father."

The group agreed to stay one night in the village, but insisted they all sleep in the same room. After what they'd been through in Hades, and after Darko found out Alikan Village was gone, none of them wanted to be apart for even a second.

They were shown to an empty bedroom with a single window on the second floor of Chief Agni's cabin, then given blankets and pillows. They made themselves each a bed on the floor so they'd be side by side.

The second Diana's head hit the pillow, she fell asleep. Darko tossed and turned for a bit, but eventually began to snore. Zoey closed her eyes and drifted off for a while, then woke with a start to Andy's muffled sobs.

She sat up and looked around the dark, empty bedroom, lit by a sliver of moonlight as it poked through the window. Andy was nowhere to be seen, but she could hear him as he cried.

"Andy?" she whispered, trying not to wake Diana and Darko. "Where are you?" He appeared beside her, the Helm of Darkness in his hands. His lip quivered, his eyes red and puffy. "What are you doing? What's wrong?" she asked.

He sat in front of her and rested the Helm in the space between them. "Remember what the Fates said about the Helm—that whoever wields it can see all the souls that reside in Hades or whatever?" he whispered.

Zoey's heart sank. She didn't like where this was going. "What about it?"

"I couldn't stop thinking about my family. When Persephone asked me to join her— I mean, I almost did it. More than anything I wanted to see them again. But I knew I couldn't. I couldn't abandon you like that, Zoey. I couldn't abandon any of you." He paused, and a tear trickled down his cheek. "Well, tonight, I couldn't stop thinking about them. And I thought maybe I could see them through the Helm."

Zoey took one of his hands in her own. Dealing with Spencer's death and her lost hand had made her almost forget about Andy's act of selflessness in Hades. She'd been terrified that he would choose Persephone so he could save his family, but in the end, he'd proved her wrong. She felt terrible that he'd never get the chance to see them again—after all, it was pretty much the only reason he'd wanted to come on the quest—but she hoped that with time, he'd find comfort in knowing he'd made the right choice.

If his loved ones were watching over him, she was sure they were proud.

"Were you able to see them?" she asked.

Andy shook his head. "No. I saw a lot of dead people, but my family wasn't anywhere to be found. It's like they never existed."

Zoey smiled. "Or maybe they're not in Hades."

Andy furrowed his brow. "You think so?"

She shrugged. "I don't know what to think exactly. If the Greek gods are real, who's to say the Egyptian gods aren't? The Norse gods, the Incan gods, the Polynesian gods? Your family could be anywhere—we just don't know. After everything we've seen and been through, it seems like just about anything is possible." A lump formed in her throat. She pulled away from Andy and ran her hand over the Helm, the cold metal cooling her fingertips. Was her father in Hades?

She picked the Helm up and pulled it over her head.

Chills bolted through her, as though hundreds of ghosts were passing through her body. Once the feeling subsided, she held up her hand to her face and wiggled her fingers, but all she could see before her was empty space.

Hey, Helm? she thought. *I'd like to see my father if he's in Hades, please. His name is Antonio Moretti. Toni for short.* It felt strange to think her father's name, but it was also oddly satisfying. She'd been denying that part of her life for far too long.

Images danced before her eyes. The green hills and glittering palaces of Elysium, the dry grassland of Asphodel, the red skies and scorched landscape of the Fields of Punishment, the blue flames of Tartarus. Hundreds of faces flashed before her in rapid succession, the faces of souls wandering Hades for all eternity, but the Helm stopped for none of them, and none were her father.

Finally the images faded, and all she could see was Andy as he stared at her with wide eyes in the dark bedroom of Chief Agni's cabin. She pulled off the Helm. "My father isn't in Hades, either. I wonder if Spencer is. Hades said Syrena was burning in Tartarus."

"Why don't you look?" Andy said.

She pulled the Helm over her head, and the chilling sensation ran through her again. *Show me Spencer, the Son of Hades,* she commanded. *And Syrena, the Daughter of Poseidon.* The same landscapes and more faces danced before her eyes, but the Helm stopped for nothing, not even as it passed through Tartarus. Eventually she was returned to the bedroom again.

She took off the Helm, her eyes filling with tears. Andy took her hand. "Did you see him?" he asked.

She smiled with quivering lips. "No. He's not there. And neither is Syrena. I can't help but think that . . . that . . ."

Andy squeezed her hand. "That they're some place better?" She nodded.

There was a knock on the window. Zoey jumped and looked over. Kali was outside, on the back of a pegasus with a black coat and green eyes, a pack of supplies slung behind her. Ajax and Aladdin were on either side of them, happily flapping their wings.

Andy rushed to the window and threw it open. "Kali? What are you doing?"

Kali smirked. "Isn't it obvious? I'm coming with you. I can't let you have all the fun, slaying monsters and taking down gods."

His jaw dropped. "How'd you convince your father to let you come with us?"

"I didn't. He's asleep. Wake those two up. It's time to go." Zoey began shaking Diana and Darko awake.

"How are we going to get around all the guards?" Andy asked. "All the watchtowers?"

"We'll sneak past them," Kali said with a shrug. Diana and Darko sat up and yawned, and when Diana caught sight of Kali, she rubbed her widened eyes as if in disbelief. "Get up, Princess. It's time to go."

Diana shook her head. "If you leave, your dad will come after us."

"He won't catch us if we hurry," Kali said.

Diana huffed. "Fine." Zoey grinned and gave Andy a high five. Darko beamed.

Kali introduced her green-eyed pegasus as Luna, whom she'd "borrowed" from her friend Dev. In her pack were a couple of spears she'd taken, safely secured.

"We have the Helm and Medusa's head," Zoey said. "What now? How are we going to reach Poseidon's palace?"

"I'm not sure yet. It's deep in the ocean," Diana said. "For now we'll head toward the twelve cities. From there we'll steal whatever we may need and figure out a way into the palace." They all nodded in reply.

Zoey and Diana climbed onto Aladdin's back, while Andy and Darko hoisted themselves onto Ajax. Together, they soared into the night.

* ~ * ~ * ~

After Diana, Andy, and Zoey disappeared from Hades, Karter stayed with Spencer. He cried, he screamed. He kicked the pile of bones around the room. He tore Persephone's throne of wildflowers and vines to shreds. Once he calmed, he cradled Spencer's head in his lap, praying to whatever god was listening to have mercy on Spencer's soul.

He had no idea how much time had passed, but eventually the Furies began to regenerate, their flesh melding back together, their bones cracking into place. Before they could fully heal themselves, Karter let out a final defeated sob and bid Spencer farewell, then closed his eyes and took a bite of the golden apple.

When he opened his eyes again, he'd escaped Hades and was sitting outside the entrance. He wandered for a while, lost in the fog, the cold night air numbing his wounds. His chest burned. His body had been pushed past the point of exhaustion. He looked up at the stars, searching for Asteria, trying to call for her, but his throat was so parched he couldn't get the words out.

Where was she? She'd told him to go to Hades, that if he did, he could save Spencer. He'd done what she said, and still, Spencer was dead. As a goddess of prophetic dreams, had she known that was his true fate? Or had she just made a mistake?

A few tears slipped down his cheeks, despair overcoming him. He had nothing to live for. Syrena and Spencer were dead. Asteria was nowhere to be found. If his father found out what he'd done, he'd surely be executed. His knees buckled. He fell face-first onto the rocky ground, his vision going black.

When he woke, he found himself sprawled on the floor of a small cave, the moon shining on his clammy, feverish face.

He sat up in panic. How much time had passed? How

had he arrived there? Had his father discovered what happened? Had Hades and Persephone managed to escape Tartarus and regenerate themselves?

Three dark figures stepped into the cave, blocking the light of the moon. "And the Son of Zeus awakens," the familiar, seductive voice of a young woman said.

Karter peered at the figures, his eyesight adjusting to the dark. "Violet? Is that you?"

The young woman laughed and approached him, her wavy blonde locks bouncing against her hips. She was as tall as he, her slender tan frame dressed with peach robes. She puckered her lips and blew him a kiss, her opalescent eyes glittering pink and green and silver even in the dark.

Karter clenched his jaw and avoided her gaze. If one looked too long at Violet—a very easy thing to do—and if she willed it, if they didn't already have strong feelings for someone else, they fell madly in love with her. As a Daughter of Aphrodite, the Goddess of Love and Beauty herself, she'd discovered over time it was her most useful power.

At one time, Karter and Violet had dated. He'd fallen in love with her. Whether it was for the real her or because of her child-of-Aphrodite powers, he had no idea, but nevertheless, he'd fallen in love with her. After he'd attained his scar, she'd broken it off with him. She'd said he was a shame to the demigods of Olympus, and there was no point in surrounding herself with ugly, unlovable things like scars.

"You look awful, Karter," Violet said. "More awful than I've ever seen. It's sad. You used to be so handsome."

Karter snorted. "Glad you noticed." A wave of intense nausea hit him, his vision spinning. He cupped his forehead. "I feel worse than I ever have, too. What's going on?"

The other two figures stepped toward Karter. The first was a young woman a bit shorter and stouter than Violet, with a bush of tight burgundy coils piled atop her head. Layla, Daughter of Ares, God of War. Then a muscular young man, the shortest of the bunch, with dark-olive skin, smooth black hair, and a crooked smile. Xander, Son of Hermes, Messenger of the Gods.

Layla smirked. "We found you nearly dead close to the entrance of Hades."

"But what are you doing all the way out here?" Karter said.

"We're on a mission for Zeus, naturally," Violet said. "With Syrena dead and you and Spencer on the lookout for Diana, our team was the next in line to go."

Karter groaned, his stomach churning. "My wounds . . . I'm . . ."

"You're dying of infection," Xander said. "But Zeus wants you in Olympus alive, so we have to hurry and get you there."

"What? Zeus wants— But why?"

Layla chuckled. "He knows what you did in Hades. We all do. The Furies contacted him after it happened. And now it's our job to take you back."

Karter's heart sank. His father knew what he'd done, and soon he'd be executed, joining Syrena and Spencer in death. What had become of their souls, and what would become of his? He turned away from his fellow demigods and retched.

* ~ * ~ * ~

The group soared across the pink clouds of a golden sunrise, over Andy and Zoey's destroyed city.

The sight made Andy think of his best friend, his sister, his mother, his father, and Spencer. Although he missed them more than he could express, the memory of them filled him with soothing warmth. He couldn't see them, even through the Helm, but that was okay. He'd be all right. They'd always be a part of him, even in death. He couldn't save them, but maybe he could save the rest of the world.

He hoped to make them proud.

He looked over at Zoey, who watched the debris pass below as she clung to Diana on the back of Aladdin. *Soon*, he thought. *I'll tell her how I feel.* Her gaze met his, and she gave him a tired smile, her brilliant blue eyes shining in the sunrise.

To be continued in the second installment of the War on the Gods trilogy . . .

POSEIDON'S TRIDENT

A. P. Mobley is a young-adult fantasy author, her debut novel being *The Helm of Darkness*. She grew up in Wyoming and currently lives there. She considers herself a huge nerd, loves chocolate a little too much, and plays with her hamster, Marceline (nicknamed Marcy), into late hours of the night.

Follow her on Twitter and Instagram: @author_apmobley.

Make sure to leave *The Helm of Darkness* a review on Amazon and Goodreads!

ACKNOWLEDGEMENTS

I want to give a massive thanks to all the people who had a part in my journey.

Dillan, my writing buddy and good friend, thank you for being so patient with me. You gave me honest and constructive feedback, and you encouraged me when I felt like giving up. Without you I would not be the writer I am today.

Thank you to my family, for always teaching me to follow my dreams, and for encouraging me to never give up. Your love has given me courage to reach for the stars.

Cody, although we aren't together anymore, I can't *not* thank you for the help you gave me. You read the first draft and encouraged me to keep working on it. You have no idea how much that helped. It forced me to keep going when I felt I had nothing left in me.

Nikki Mentges, my wonderful editor, thank you for not only pointing out what could be improved and giving me tips on how to do so, but also for telling me what was done well. That pushed me to just do better and better. Your hard work was pivotal in the completion of the final version of this story.

Thank you, Gabrielle Ragusi, the incredible artist who did the cover and promotional images for this book. You are so talented, and I can't imagine anyone else having done the artwork. You brought my visions to life in a way I don't think anyone else could.

A big thank you to Cloud Kitten Publishing for taking on this book's interior design. You guys might be just starting out, but you do stunning work. I know you'll go far.

Thank you, Jason and Angie Plett, the lovely couple who took my author photo. Your photography gets better with every new picture I see, and I appreciate the time and care you put into taking my photo.

Jenna Moreci, you are an insanely talented author, I absolutely love your work, and I want to thank you for your writing advice on YouTube. I can honestly say this story would not be where it is today without your helpful videos. You are one of my greatest inspirations, and one of my heroes.

Lastly, thank you, dear Reader, for giving *The Helm of Darkness* a chance. I hope it took you on a fantastical adventure you enjoyed every second of.